You may renew this loan for a further period by phone, letter,
personal visit or at www.kirklees.gov.uk/libraries, provided
that the book is not required by another reader.

NO MORE THAN THREE RENEWALS ARE PERMITTED

W70

Laura reached for a piece of toast and took her coffee with her.

She had an hour before the first guests would arrive, and she was going to enjoy it with Cody and Johnny.

Johnny insisted on putting on his cowboy boots and his cowboy hat. He said that he wanted "to look just like Mr. Masters."

Oh, you do, my little boy. You do.

Laura walked past all the tables with Johnny. She had to admit everything looked beautiful. Where she would be sitting, at the head table, she'd have a perfect view of the barn. Maybe she could catch glimpses of Cody and Johnny during the riding lesson.

As Laura and Johnny approached the barn, Cody appeared, leading Pirate into the corral.

Johnny waved excitedly. "Hi, Mr. Masters. Hi, Pirate."

"Hello, son," Cody replied, and Laura's heart did a flip in her chest at that simple greeting, which had much more meaning now.

The Rancher's Surprise Son

CHRISTINE WENGER

First published in Great Britain 2015
by Mills & Boon, an imprint of Harlequin (UK) Limited,
Large Print edition 2015
Eton House, 18-24 Paradise Road,
Richmond, Surrey, TW9 1SR

© 2015 Christine Wenger

ISBN: 978-0-263-26004-5

Harlequin (UK) Limited's policy is to use papers that are natural, renewable and recyclable products and made from wood grown in sustainable forests. The logging and manufacturing processes conform to the legal environmental regulations of the country of origin.

Printed and bound in Great Britain
by CPI Antony Rowe, Chippenham, Wiltshire

CHRISTINE WENGER

has worked in the criminal justice field for more years than she cares to remember, but now she spends her time reading, writing and seeing the sights in our beautiful world. A native central New Yorker, she loves watching professional bull riding and rodeo with her favorite cowboy, her husband, Jim. You can reach Chris at PO Box 1823, Cicero, NY 13039, or through her website at christinewenger.com.

For all cowboys and cowgirls
everywhere—in the country,
the suburbs and in the city.
(You know who you are!)

Chapter One

As far as Laura Duke knew, no Duke vehicle had ever left a tread on the Masters family's Double M Ranch...until now.

It started out to be a perfectly normal day, whatever "normal" meant. Since nothing had been normal for the past several years, Laura was enjoying the quiet respite of visiting with her son Johnny's babysitter, Cindy Masters, at the nearby Double M.

In a cloud of Arizona desert dust, one of the

Duke Ranch's white pickups came lumbering down the road.

"That looks like one of your trucks," Cindy said. "I've always loved the crown on the side. I told my mom that the Double M needs a cool logo like yours."

"A crown for a duke," Laura answered. More like a king, she thought. *Since my father rules the entire county.*

Laura loved Cindy and so did Laura's son, Johnny. Cindy was a wonderful babysitter, but Laura asked her to sit only when she was in a jam, like this Friday. She had to speak at an awards luncheon, and her parents would be out of town. Clarissa, Johnny's nanny, had that day off.

"Sure. I'd love to watch Johnny again," thirteen-year-old Cindy said. "He's the cutest."

Laura was relieved, but if her parents knew she was at the Double M and Cindy was babysitting Johnny, there'd be hell to pay.

Laura's heart raced thinking that if her parents even suspected that she was good friends with Georgianna Masters, Cindy's mom, and enjoyed her company, they'd really flip. Well, her mother would definitely flip, but her father seemed to have a well-hidden soft spot for Georgianna.

Still, Laura had her reasons for risking the wrath of her parents—good reasons—reasons that she'd been keeping to herself for a long time.

The screen door of the porch squeaked open, and Georgianna walked out onto the porch.

"Cody? Is that Cody coming in the Duke truck?" Georgianna asked, wiping her hands on a terry towel. "Oh, thank goodness. He's finally here!"

The pickup was still making its way toward the front of the ranch house, and Laura found herself holding her breath.

Why on earth would Cody Masters be riding in a Duke truck?

More important, how did he get out of prison?

"Is it really him?" Cindy asked, straining her neck. "Three years. I haven't seen my brother in three years."

Three years and four days, to be exact.

Georgianna took Cindy's hand. "It sure is Cody, sweetie. He's home."

Laura's heart beat wildly in her chest. She felt warm, then chilled, then as if she was frying under the desert sun in spite of the shady roof overhead.

She knew that this day would come sooner or later and dreaded it—yet she couldn't wait to see Cody again.

So many secrets. So many lies. So much heartbreak.

Georgianna and Cindy took off at a run to meet the truck.

Laura stayed in the shade, holding back.

The scenario that she had planned when she first talked to Cody—*really* talked to Cody—seemed ridiculous now. She needed to think!

The pickup slowed, and then stopped. Laura willed herself to run, to hide, but she was rooted in that spot. She needed to delay seeing Cody until she had a better plan—and it sure as hell had better be a great one.

Procrastination might as well be her middle name.

Holding back, she mentally called herself a supreme coward, and watched as Cody swung his long legs from the passenger side of the pickup, stood, then swept his mother into his arms. He swung her in circles as she shrieked in happiness.

"Yee-haw!" Cody's deep voice echoed across his mother's little pie-slice of property that was smack-dab in the middle of the Duke holdings.

Cody finally put his mother down, walked

over to Cindy and hugged her close. "How's my little sis?"

"Oh, Cody! I've missed you. Have you been okay in jail? I mean, really okay? I can't believe you wouldn't let us visit you."

"It wasn't a place for ladies, but I loved your letters. I looked forward to them every day. You're quite the writer."

"I know," Cindy said, grinning. "I want to be an author when I'm older."

Cody kissed her on the forehead. "You can do whatever you want, sis. Don't you ever think you can't."

Tears sprang to Laura's eyes. She wished her family could be this close, but it never seemed that her father, the rich and powerful J. W. Duke, had time for her or her mother. The only one who he dropped everything for was her son.

She couldn't stop staring at Cody. He looked older and pale. The slump in his shoulders made him seem…defeated, maybe. Or sad. Or maybe he was just tired.

The foreman of the Duke Ranch emerged from the driver's side of the pickup. She'd always liked Slim Gonzalez. He was one of the few who could handle her father.

"I'm supposed to take Cody straight to the Duke Ranch," he said with a slight accent. "But I thought he should stop here quickly to see his family and get a change of clothes."

Cody clamped Slim's shoulder. "Let me take a shower. I promise I'll hurry. I need to get this jail stink off me. *Por favor, mi amigo.*"

"Okay," Slim nodded. "But hurry up. Remember that you and I have an appointment with J.W. and your parole officer in J.W.'s office."

Georgianna suddenly turned toward her. "Oh! I forgot. Laura is here." She waved at her, and Laura lifted her hand in return.

"Hi, Cody. Welcome home," Laura said,

trying to keep her voice calm and even, but she could hear her anxiety in those four short words.

Cody turned toward her, and she knew the second his turquoise-blue eyes found her on the porch. Those eyes could turn as cold as the sky on a frosty day or as warm as a hot day in summer.

Today they were warm.

"Laura." He smiled. "It's really good to see you."

She knew she was staring at him, but he was staring at her, too. He didn't move, and didn't say another word.

Laura remembered the shirt and suit that he was wearing now. He'd worn it on one of their last dates at the fancy restaurant in town and again on that horrible day in county court when he was sentenced and two burly deputies took him away in it.

It was way too big on him now.

Laura had never thought he was guilty, never. Her Cody wouldn't hurt a fly. He was gentle with both animals and children, and he was sweet to Cindy and protective of Cindy and his mother.

But the criminal justice system proved her wrong and had found him guilty. Maybe it was because he wouldn't defend himself, even when his public defender pointed out that he couldn't provide him with adequate representation. Cody remained mute throughout the proceedings, insisting that he just wanted to plead guilty and do his time.

He'd gotten his wish. Now Cody was a felon. He'd been convicted of some kind of manslaughter for killing Georgianna's second husband, Hank Lindy.

The same smarmy Hank Lindy who hit on her during a shopping trip to his store while he was married to Georgianna.

The slime. Of course, she never told Georgianna, but she had avoided Lindy like the Ebola virus.

In her heart of hearts, she still believed her Cody would never kill anyone, but she wanted to hear it from him—and soon. He just had to be protecting someone, but whom?

Just like before, Cody might not talk about what had happened that awful night when Hal Lindy had been fatally shot, even though Laura had begged him constantly to defend himself. All her pleas fell on deaf ears.

But now that he was released, maybe she could talk him into giving up his secrets.

Slim cleared his throat and broke the silence, along with their eye contact. "You'd better get a move on, Cody."

Cody nodded and slipped one arm around his mother and the other around Cindy. Everyone would have to go past Laura to enter the ranch house. She couldn't escape now.

Cody reached out and was about to touch her

hair, but he stopped. "Laura, can you stay for a while? Can we talk?"

It'd been years since the prison officials took Cody away. No matter how much she begged, he wouldn't put her on his visitors' list. She wasn't much of a letter writer, but she'd sent him one a week at first, telling him about how Georgianna and Cindy were doing, hoping to ease his mind about them.

But after a while, there was nothing she'd wanted to say, so she wrote less frequently.

God help her. She wanted to run to Cody and feel herself in his arms again. She'd always felt safe with him and always loved.

Safe? With a killer?

Instead, she shook her head and prayed that Slim wouldn't tell her father that she'd been at the Double M. "Sorry, I have to get going."

"Will I see you soon?" Cody asked quietly. "Our place?"

She nodded. He did the same. That was all

she was going to get for now, and that simple gesture was all she could give in return.

Georgianna gave Laura a quick peck on the cheek. "Come and visit again," she said, following Cody inside.

Cindy turned back and waved to her as she walked on the squeaky, splintered boards of the porch. "Bye, Laura. See you on Friday when you drop Johnny off."

Laura's breath caught in her throat at the mention of her son. She hoped Cody hadn't heard what Cindy had said, not until she had a chance to think things through.

She'd thought she'd had another two years before she had to worry about telling Cody about Johnny.

But her time was up. Cody wasn't stupid.

She was hard-pressed to make something positive out of this situation that had suddenly been thrust upon her. It was easier to procrastinate and believe that Cody's felony conviction and incarceration hadn't happened.

Laura waved goodbye to Cindy and noticed that Slim took a seat on the rocking chair on the porch to wait for him.

"Slim, what's going on?" Laura asked when the Masters family was inside the ranch house. "I didn't know that Cody was being released today."

"I just found out, too. Your father apparently arranged for his early release. This morning he told me that Cody was going to get out early and to go pick him up at the correctional facility."

"Wait a second." Laura raised a hand like a traffic cop. "My father helped to get Cody out on parole?"

"*Sí.*"

"I don't understand. My father was never a Cody Masters fan."

Slim removed his straw hat and hung it on a

knee. "That's putting it mildly. All I know is that Georgianna Masters—er… I mean, Georgianna *Lindy*—paid the boss a visit, and soon the parole people were talking to J.W. So this morning, J.W. told me that after I pick Cody up, he's going to be working at the Duke Ranch as part of his parole."

Interesting, Laura thought. *I wonder what Daddy is up to.*

"But Cody's own ranch needs a lot of work," Laura said. "It's been going downhill since he went to prison. He should be able to work his own property, not my father's! Georgianna is struggling to keep it up herself, and Cindy has to go to school."

"Cody's worked both ranches before." Slim shrugged. "And from what I understand, the wages that he earned at J.W.'s back then went toward fixing up the Double M. As long as prison didn't break Cody's back, he can do the same again."

The Dukes had always had so much, and the Masters family barely scraped by. As far back as Laura could remember, it had been like that. To make things worse, her father enjoyed constantly riding Cody, telling him that he, Georgianna and Cindy would be better off if they sold their ranch back to J.W.

Maybe for once her father was right.

It'd be difficult avoiding Cody because, as exes, he knew they had things to discuss, but she'd have to avoid him as much as possible until she figured out a plan.

"Slim, what will his duties be?"

"According to J.W., I'm to treat him like a typical greenhorn. He can start by mucking out the stalls."

Laura sighed. It wasn't just Cody that her father disliked. It always stuck in his craw that Mike Masters, Cody's father, had won his little pie-slice of land, along with a decaying farmhouse from J.W., in an all-night drunken poker game.

Subsequently, J.W. had devoted his life to getting the land back.

To that end, he was probably going to use Cody somehow. Maybe use him to influence Georgianna Masters to sell out. That was the kind of man J.W. was. It was his way or the highway.

Secrets. She'd have to keep hers as long as she could.

Cody shook off his rumpled suit and hurried into the shower, letting the water sluice over him. It couldn't be hot enough, as far as he was concerned.

A private shower—what a luxury! He fingered the vinyl curtain with a school of tropical fish swimming over a coral reef. He laughed at the design on a curtain in the middle of the damn Arizona desert.

As the bathroom filled up with steam, he took a deep breath and poured shower gel all over himself. Then he found a pink loofah and scraped his skin with it until it tingled.

As soon as he had a block of time, he'd head up into the mountains—to Saguaro Canyon— and soak in the cold rushing water. He knew just the spot, too. It was a favorite of his and Laura's.

They used to sit in the creek for hours at a time, his arm around her shoulders and her head on his chest. They'd relax in comfortable silence, just enjoying each other's company. Sometimes they'd talk about the future. It had always been their dream that somehow he'd make his mark in the world and then he'd ask J.W. for her hand in marriage.

But now he was a jailbird, a convicted felon. No one in their right mind would hire him, much less let him marry their daughter, but he knew he'd made the right decision, and he'd have to live with the consequences.

He supposed he should be grateful that he had a paying job at J.W.'s ranch and that he got out of that hellhole earlier than he'd thought he would, even though he'd planned on serving his whole sentence. There were just some things that a man had to do to protect those he loved.

He soaped up again and kept scrubbing with the loofah. Then he washed his hair with mango-coconut shampoo that must have been his mother's or sister's, digging his fingernails into his scalp.

For the next several minutes, he just stood under the spray, letting the hot water cleanse his body, cleanse his soul.

With a sigh of regret, he turned it off.

He couldn't stall any longer. He was burning daylight.

He'd just spent three years out of five for involuntary manslaughter, and he owed the parole system two more years. That meant two years working as an indentured servant for J. W. Duke.

In his wildest dreams, he could never imagine that he'd be working for J.W., and that he'd even pull some strings and get Cody out of jail early.

He sighed. The fact that his stepfather, Hank Lindy, would never hurt another woman again was one of the things that had made Cody's incarceration tolerable. If there truly was a heaven and hell, Lindy's soul was in the special kind of hell reserved for those who hit women, nearly killing them, and who preyed on young girls.

From all appearances, Hank Lindy, the owner of a feed and farm equipment store, was the epitome of a model citizen. That was the Lindy that his mother decided to marry. Cody never asked her if she'd really loved him, or just thought that he'd be generous and help get the Double M back into the black.

Georgianna had been very wrong.

While incarcerated, Cody had met a handful of genuinely great guys. Guilt, innocence or hard luck aside, they became his salvation. They got him through three damn years of hell, and he couldn't have survived without them.

Nor could he have survived without the picture of Laura Duke that he'd taped to the filthy cinder-block wall in his cell. The picture reminded him of better times—riding horses with her through the fields, Laura cheering for him at high school football games, going with her to the junior and senior proms.

Of course, they'd had to sneak around to see each other, and Cody hated the deception, but J.W. had forbidden his beautiful daughter—his only child—to date him.

Even though they'd grown up next to one another and had gone to the same schools, Cody

Masters had never been good enough for Laura in J.W.'s mind. He didn't come from a well-off family and he wasn't connected financially, socially or politically.

Then there was the fact that he was the son of Mike Masters.

The bad blood between J.W. and Mike Masters was legendary in Duke Springs. Rumor had it that years ago, J.W. wanted to marry Georgianna, but Mike had beat him to her. His mother always had a special feeling for J.W., Cody knew that, but she always denied that she would have married anyone but Mike Masters.

And when J.W. had lost the land in that drunken poker game and had wanted to buy it back throughout the years, well, their feud became epic.

Cody flashed back to the summer day, years ago, that he'd first worked up enough courage to ask Laura to go riding with him. He was about Cindy's age at the time.

"Cody, I want to talk to you." J.W. had sat him down on a hay bale in the barn and had pointed a finger at him. "You have nothing to offer Laura. I don't want you to knock on the door of my house until you do, and even then, I might not open it to you. And if I find that you are sneaking around behind my back with her...well, you'd better be prepared for the consequences."

But he'd gone against J.W.'s wishes and went behind his back to see Laura, just as he always had. In school, it was easy. Out of school, they both had to be even sneakier, and it went against his moral grain.

He remembered moving Laura into her dorm room at the University of Arizona in Phoenix. She'd been excited and eager to start her new life away from the Duke Ranch and away from her father's immediate control. She'd had the sweet taste of freedom on her soft, warm lips and hot body, and they'd made love for the first time.

It was a day he'd never forget.

And he'd never forget today, either, seeing Laura for the first time in three years. Damn, she looked better than ever. She'd let her blond, silky hair grow and it fell over her shoulders in shades of gold. Shiny bangs tickled her eyebrows, but it was her eyes that told him everything. As he passed by, they looked him over, from the top of his cowboy hat to the bottom of his old boots and the silly suit he wore. He could see the sadness in her eyes.

Did she still love him?

Her letters had been his lifeline. At first, she'd written him every day, begging him to let her visit him, but he steadfastly refused. He didn't want her to see him in there, but more importantly, he was afraid that she'd catch him at a weak moment, and he'd spill his guts.

She'd been mad, and her letters only came

once a week. She claimed that she was hurt and claimed that there was nothing happening to tell him.

He always wrote her back immediately, but he'd sent the letters to the Double M. He knew that his mother would see that Laura got them, just as sure as he knew that J.W. or Laura's mother, Penny, would destroy them.

He and Laura had made such wonderful plans for their future, but there was no chance now, no future for them.

He didn't want to saddle Laura with a jailbird.

Before everything happened, they'd had plans to leave Duke Springs and relocate to escape the long-reaching claws of J.W.

As he toweled himself off, Cody looked out the window. His gaze was drawn to the logo of the Duke Ranch on the side of the white pickup. J.W. had a fleet of new white vehicles. The Double M had a beat-up ten-year-old

Dodge Ram that was on a respirator. Once red, it was now pink from sunburn.

Cody stared at the crown—a perfect representation of J.W.'s character. Along with the Duke Ranch, the man owned all of Duke Springs—the bank, some clothing and shoe stores, the grocery, the feed and tractor store. Everything was a spoke in J.W.'s far-reaching wheel.

Everything, except the Double M.

As Cody slipped into a pair of worn jeans he'd found in his dresser and an equally worn black T-shirt, he found himself itching to get back to ranch work. But he wished it was his own property that he'd be working on. The Duke Ranch wasn't where he wanted to be. Not today. Not any day.

He had to admit that at the Duke Ranch, he could see Laura from time to time. That was something to look forward to, but they'd have to be careful and tiptoe around so they could talk, catch up and maybe salvage some of their plans.

That is, if Laura still wanted him. He couldn't read her today. She seemed shocked to see him. Hadn't J.W. told Laura that her father had helped to get Cody paroled?

He wouldn't blame her if she didn't want anything to do with him. At the start of his incarceration, her letters told him that she still loved him, but the frequency of her letters had faded. When she did write him, it was mostly about his mother and sister and nothing personal about Laura herself.

He told himself for the hundredth time that Laura must have moved on and that anything between them was over.

He didn't blame her one bit. He'd told her to forget him and find someone else.

But damn, he'd really hoped she hadn't listened to him.

Chapter Two

"Laura's little boy, Johnny, is a hoot. He's going to be quite the cowboy when he grows up." Slim Gonzalez handed Cody a pitchfork later that afternoon in one of the huge barns on the Duke Ranch. "You should see the little guy on his pony, Pirate."

Cody's mouth went dry. He plopped down on a hay bale before he fell over. Grabbing a bottle of cold water from his small cooler, he took a long draw, then poured the rest over the back of his neck.

Cody turned toward Slim and braced himself. He wanted—no, *needed*—more information.

"Laura has a son?" Cody's heart thumped as he spoke to Slim and one of the other Duke Ranch hands listened in. "Tell me more."

"His name is Johnny. He's three, maybe almost four years old."

Why didn't she wait for me?

Cody took another long drink. He didn't want to ask his next question, but he had to know. "Did Laura get married?"

"To a guy she met at college. From what I hear, it didn't last long. Too bad. She deserves more."

Cody tried to let that all sink in. Laura got married and had a son with her husband. He fumed at another man touching her, making love to her.

He'd always thought of Laura as his. She gave her virginity to him in her small dorm room on a twin bed, and she'd told him that she'd loved him since first grade. He'd echoed that same statement, and told her that someday he'd make her father proud. Someday he'd make something out of himself and could date her out in the open, not sneak around behind J.W.'s back.

It was selfish of him, but even when he told her to forget him—to find someone else—he'd hoped like hell that Laura would wait for him until he was released from prison. Three years was probably a long time, but here he was, ready to pick up where they'd left off.

Shoot. She must have found someone right away.

For a second, he wondered if the little boy was his, but then shrugged it off. In her letters, Laura certainly would have told him that he was going to be a father. Wouldn't she? Of course she would!

Cody couldn't wait to see Laura alone and

ask her about the college dude. He wondered if she was divorced or still married to the guy.

Dammit, why the hell did she marry someone else?

He had to leave, get out of here. The huge barn felt as small as his jail cell. He jogged outside and sat on an overturned barrel behind the building, gulping the hot desert air.

Where was Laura? He had to talk to her.

Laura, her mother, J.W. and Johnny sat on designer chairs on the flagstone patio that was surrounded on three sides by the wings of the Duke ranch house. They were shaded from the hot sun by a large pergola, rich with bright fuchsia bougainvillea and surrounded by natural desert flora and fauna.

Laura loved moments like this—nice and easy, when she could enjoy the company of her family—that was, until someone started a fight.

She took a tray from Clarissa, Johnny's nanny and all-around helper, which contained a frosty blown-glass pitcher and four matching pale green glasses that she'd bought on a trip to Mexico. Laura had always loved the set, and liked looking at the tiny bubbles that seemed to be trapped inside the thick glass.

"Thanks, Clarissa," Laura said then turned to her father. "I hear you hired Cody Masters, Dad."

He took the pitcher from the tray and poured the lemonade into a glass. "News travels fast."

"Did you also help him get out on parole?" Laura asked, trying to be nonchalant.

"I did." He tickled Johnny, and the laughing boy climbed out of his booster seat and got comfortable on his grandfather's lap. J.W. hugged him tightly.

Johnny just adored his grandfather, and Laura could tell by J.W.'s various questions and comments to the boy that the man was training him to take over the Duke Ranch.

Johnny was the son that J.W. had never had.

"What your father didn't tell you was that Georgianna Lindy walked over here and asked him to get Cody out." Her mother glared at J.W. "The man killed someone, and your father gets him out of jail because she came and smiled at him."

Her mother's old wounds never healed. Penelope Belcher Duke had always despised Georgianna Masters Lindy. The story went way back and added to the long discord between J.W. and Mike Masters.

The truth was that J.W. loved Georgianna first, but she'd picked Mike Masters over him, and Penny never stopped feeling like second best.

"That's enough, Penny," J.W. said between gritted teeth.

"Grandpa, can I ride Pirate now?" Johnny asked.

"No. Not right now, honey," Laura answered. "It's time for your nap."

"Grandpa, I want to ride my horse!"

"Aw, Laura, let the boy ride. He's a genuine Duke," J.W. said. "He loves horses."

"As opposed to a counterfeit Duke?" Laura said under her breath. "Dad, remember that I'm Johnny's mother, and what I say goes. Please don't interfere."

"Oh, all right," J.W. snapped at her, then turned to Johnny and tickled him. "Do what your mother says." J.W. lifted Johnny and set him on the flagstones. "Take your nap, partner, and then you can ride your horse."

Just as Laura stood up to take Johnny to his bedroom, Clarissa appeared and extended her hand. With a glance back at J.W., Johnny put his hand in Clarissa's. "I'll be right back, Grandpa."

J.W. grinned and lit a cigar. "Sweet dreams, Johnny."

Sweet dreams? Too bad she'd never heard J.W. say that to her when she was Johnny's age. Laura followed Clarissa and Johnny toward the ranch house, feeling like a third wheel.

J.W. reached out and clasped Laura's wrist. "Wait a minute. I want to talk to you," her father said in the gruff tone he reserved for Laura and her mother.

"Yes?" Laura anticipated a pounding headache and sat back down. She looked to her mother for assistance, but Penny was busy typing something on her cell phone.

J.W. took a long pull on his cigar and blew a stream of stinky smoke into the bougainvillea. "I want to talk to you about Cody Masters."

"I figured you would, sooner or later." Laura knew the drill. "I'll avoid him as much as I can, Dad, but what do you want me to do? Cody's working here at the ranch, and I live and work here. I take Johnny to the barn to ride and out for walks. I'm bound to run into Cody."

"You know what I mean."

"You've been telling me the same thing since I was a kid. Cody Masters isn't your enemy. Even Mike Masters wasn't your enemy. He was your good friend at one time." She turned to her mother. "Georgianna Masters was your friend at one time, too."

"That was long ago." Penny never looked up from her cell phone.

"Life is short." Laura tapped a finger on the patio table. "All the more reason why you should mend fences."

"Georgianna's the one who should mend her fence. It looks horrible. It's all falling apart."

That was her mother's attempt to change the subject and zing Georgianna at the same time, but Laura wasn't going to fall for it.

"Mom, stop."

"It's not my fault that she can't afford to keep up her so-called ranch!" her mother said.

J.W. put his cigar down. "That's enough, Penny."

"Not before I remind you that we lost that land because you got drunk and failed to win a poker game against Mike Masters. I still can't believe it."

Same old same old.

Her mother never missed an opportunity to bring up J.W.'s fateful Texas Hold 'em game thirty-something years ago. It was like a recording that played ad nauseam.

A bell on Penny's cell phone rang, indicating a text message. Penny picked up the phone, punched some buttons and read the screen.

Her mother had always been unhappy, and a lot of it had to do with the Masters family, but even more had to do with J.W. Laura always wondered why her mother didn't just didn't pack up and leave, but Laura knew that

Penny just loved being the Lady Astor of Duke Springs.

Penny pointed at the Double M, just beyond the tree line to the west of the ranch house. "That place is an eyesore."

"Mom, maybe she doesn't have the money or the help to fix it up."

J.W. rolled his cigar tip on the lip of an ashtray. "Then she should sell it back to me. Matter of fact, I suggested that when she came to see me about getting Cody out."

Laura's stomach lurched. She knew the power that J.W. wielded. "Dad, you didn't get Cody out on the condition that Georgianna sell the Double M to you, did you?"

Penny's face lit up like a Christmas tree. "Did you do that, J.W.?"

He took a long draw on his cigar. "I have some scruples, no matter what you both think."

Laura's face flushed with guilt. Her parents didn't have a clue that the Duke Foundation had provided Georgianna with money to do some repairs to her ranch house.

And Laura was in charge of the Duke Foundation!

There would be hell to pay if one of them ever found out, but Laura was satisfied that she'd covered her tracks. Also, Georgianna didn't know that she was getting Duke money, or she'd definitely have refused it. Laura convinced Georgianna that she was receiving grant money earmarked for the preservation of historic ranches, and the Double M qualified.

Stubbornness. Who needed it?

Laura shifted in her chair. She didn't like all the deception, but what else was she to do? She wanted to help Georgianna. Indirectly, she was helping Cody and Cindy.

"Cody's back, so he'll help his mother get the ranch going."

"Oh no he won't. I'll keep him so busy, he won't have time to work his ranch," J.W. hissed.

"Dad, how can you be so hateful?"

"The boy will be so damn exhausted, he'll realize that he can't handle both."

Laura felt tears of frustration stinging her eyes. "He'll quit here to work the Double M. I would."

"But he can't." J.W. grinned, balancing his cigar between his teeth. "It's a condition of his parole that he works here. I own him for two years. If he screws up his job at my ranch, he goes back to prison."

Penny reached over the table and placed her hand on J.W.'s. Her bright red, glittery nail polish gleamed in the light. "Now, that's the J.W. that I know! Cody certainly will fail. Georgianna will have no choice but to sell."

"That's my plan," J.W. said, reveling in Penny's admiration. Laura knew that he didn't get much of that from her, so he aspired to get attention and adoration from his peers and maybe from some of his ranch hands.

Laura stood. "I can't believe how cruel you both are. Cody will collapse with all the work he'll try to do. And where will Georgianna and Cindy live if you take away their home? How can you both plan something like that? Forget the stupid poker game. Forget about the Double M. Put up a fifty-foot fence if it bothers you to look at it, for heaven's sake."

Her headache was in full force and the lemonade sat sour in her stomach. How could her parents be so loving with Johnny and so hateful to the Masters family?

Laura walked toward the barn. Maybe she'd run into Cody, or at least catch a quick glimpse of him. They had so much to talk about, but first she had to warn him about her father's plan to work him to death with the hope that Cody would fail.

Although he had probably figured that out already.

She thought about her mother. Why couldn't Penny be more like Georgianna Masters Lindy? She was the grandmotherly type: loving, nurturing and so sweet to Johnny. Whenever she brought him over, Georgianna spoiled him too much—but in a good way. Laura had no doubt that Penny loved Johnny, but she didn't really show him. Laura sniffed. That was how she had been raised—at arm's length. Why should she expect anything more from her mother?

Cody and Cindy both showed love and care to Georgianna. They were three of the best people she knew. Cody and Cindy would do anything for Georgianna, and she'd do anything for them.

Laura had never been sure that her parents loved her. Her father had wanted a son to carry on the Duke Ranch legacy, so her gender was a strike against her. Instead of teaching her the ins and outs of running the ranch, her father had made sure that she did so-called "girl things" in school: ballet, baton, cheerleading. And he brought in people to give her facials, and then there were personal shoppers, and yoga instructors to teach her how to relax, but she was bored out of her mind.

J.W. was convinced that his own mother, her grandma Sarah, died from overwork. He often told stories that when his parents, Sarah and Walter Anthony Duke, first came to Duke Springs and farmed and made a ranch out of the Arizona dust, the work just killed her.

It didn't matter that Sarah died at age sixty from cancer. J.W. was convinced that it was the hard work that killed her.

J.W. took that original ranch and made it into the showplace that it was today through his own hard work and determination. He hadn't wanted Penny to work the land, cattle and horses as he had. Instead, he insisted that she occupy her time opening dress shops and gift shops—ladies' shops. Still, he didn't want his "two ladies"—neither Penny nor Laura—to ever remember how the original Duke Ranch had begun.

Laura had wanted to learn how the ranch operated, and wanted J.W. to teach her. They'd fought and fought over the years, with her father insisting that she do "woman things" instead. Fighting over this had stopped when she had Johnny. J.W. wanted a rough-and-ready boy that he could train to take over the Duke Ranch, and that was going to be her son.

Laura knew that she had to keep Johnny—and herself—away from J.W. a bit so he would not completely take over their lives.

And when she wanted to use her degree in finance to work on Wall Street, J.W. asked her if she'd run the Duke Foundation instead. He didn't want her in New York City because he'd preferred his grandson right by his side so he could make Johnny into the next version of himself.

Over her dead body.

It wasn't exactly brain surgery to give away money and let the world know that J. W. Duke was benevolent.

Actually, he was! She'd insisted that she had to live away from the ranch house, so J.W. built a cottage on the property for her and Johnny. All right, she could save money that way.

So, she'd stayed in Duke Springs, not because J.W. had asked her to, but because she'd thought that Johnny should know his family—and that included Georgianna and Cindy.

Family was everything, and she'd wanted family around Johnny.

As she walked, she remembered the original Big Upheaval. That was when she'd sat her parents down one day in the family room and told them that she was pregnant by a man at college.

Then she'd braced herself for their barrage of questions. Yes, they eloped to Vegas. No, she wasn't going to tell them his name, but he was out of the picture. Yes, she would raise their grandson alone if she wasn't welcome at home. Yes, she'd filed for divorce.

The fact that she purposely said the word *grandson* had mellowed J.W. considerably. Telling him that she was going to name the boy John Wayne Duke after him had J.W. purring like a kitten.

Laura had told them point-blank that she'd move and take Johnny away if they tried to find Johnny's father—that he wasn't in the picture at present.

But they still brought it up from time to time, and always a fight ensued.

She'd given serious thought to moving away from Duke Springs after one nasty fight with her parents that had to do with her getting support for Johnny from the man they referred to as her "college husband." Even though they believed he had run out on her, they insisted that he should be held responsible.

She told them adamantly that she wasn't going to pursue financial support and that she could provide for Johnny herself. Even when J.W. ordered her to give up his name so he could sic his lawyers on her "college husband," Laura kept reiterating that she didn't want to talk about it, or that she would move and take Johnny with her.

That never failed to quiet them down—for a while, at least.

Finally, after a particularly overwhelming fight, she'd made up a name with more vowels than consonants, and said that Johnny's father had moved to Dubai, that he wanted Johnny and her to move there to live with him.

Her parents had never brought the subject up again.

Laura stopped and looked around at the extensive Duke Ranch that went on as far as the eye could see. Little did her parents know, she could never take Johnny from them now. The little guy would miss his horse, miss the beautiful pool, the big playground made just for him and the ranch hands that just adored him. She could never take him away from her parents, from Georgianna and Cindy and now Cody.

Cody had yet to meet Johnny.

She wiped the moisture off her face with a handkerchief, took a breath and resumed her walk to the barn. To escape the tension at home and the tension churning inside her, she visited Georgianna and Cindy Masters as much as she could. It was calm at the Double M, like shelter in the middle of a storm.

As Laura turned right to the path that led to the barn, she had to admit yet again that the Duke Ranch was breathtaking in size and scope. It was surrounded by several mountain ranges, and she loved the huge saguaros that lifted their arms to the sky. She loved the lumpy prickly pear cactus with their red berries on top and the coo of the mourning doves.

The horses and cattle that dotted the hills and valleys of the ranch were prime stock, and she enjoyed looking at them.

She thought she'd seen Cody go behind the barn. Maybe, just maybe, they could have a quick conversation. She hurried down the path, watchful of her mother and father.

She needed to see him, touch him and run her fingers through his pitch-black hair that was a bit too long. She wanted to feel the warmth of his skin and feel safe and secure in his arms once again. She wanted to breathe in the special scent that was his and his alone.

It had been a long three years.

When the judge gave him five years for involuntary manslaughter, Laura gasped. Cody turned to her and said that he'd be all right.

Then she'd hurried to the ladies' room and vomited.

Walking around to the back of the barn, she saw Cody. He was just…pacing.

He must have sensed that someone was near, as he whirled around, poised for fight or flight.

"Laura?" he whispered. "Damn, don't sneak up on me like that!" He dropped his hands, hands that probably had defended him in prison. "Laura, I'm so sorry…"

Tears sprung to her eyes. "Cody. I—I… You— I…"

"I've missed you, too." They always could finish each other's sentences. "How've you been? You look…even more beautiful than…"

"I wish you would have let me visit you."

"I didn't want you to see me in there."

Laura couldn't wait any longer. She ran toward Cody, and he enveloped her in his strong arms.

Finally!

"Aw…don't cry."

"I've missed you, Cody. So very much."

"What about your husband?"

She went stiff in his arms. "How do you know about him?"

"It seems to be common knowledge among the ranch hands."

"I don't want to talk about that now, Cody. Just hold me."

"And you have a son?"

She moved back, out of his arms. She wanted to talk about her son, but not just yet; she just wanted Cody to hold her, to get to know him again. "His name is Johnny."

"Johnny." Cody nodded. "What's his last name?"

"Johnny Duke. I named him Duke."

"Did his father like that?"

"His father wasn't around when he was born, so I gave him my last name."

"I see."

"Cody, I have so much to tell you."

He looked at the mountains in the distance

as if lost in his own thoughts. "I told you not to wait for me, but I was hoping you would."

"Let's not talk about that now." She touched his arm. "Let's meet. Usual place. Usual signal. Tonight. Okay?"

"I'll be there."

"Johnny and I are living in a cottage that's to the left of the main house. The window on the right will be our signal now."

Their sign was always the half-open shade of her right bedroom window in the main house.

Actually, since the date he was sentenced, she'd never pulled the shade down on her bedroom in her cottage again. It was always raised because she was always waiting for Cody.

She'd have to be careful. She didn't want her parents, especially J.W., to find out that she was meeting him. It would be a disaster.

Besides, she didn't want to give her father any reason to send Cody back to prison.

Chapter Three

Cody slowly walked back to the remuda barn, which housed the mounts—mostly quarter horses—of the ranch hands and the Duke family.

He might as well get back to work and think about what he would say to Laura tonight without putting her on the defensive.

He probably blew it with his pointed questions, but they didn't have time for a lot of polite conversation.

He looked over into the stall of Johnny's

horse, Pirate, a cute little black-and-white pinto pony. He could almost picture Laura's son sitting in the tiny saddle as she led the horse around the paddock.

Cody wondered if the boy looked like her.

The Duke Ranch had four more barns with twenty stalls each, most of which housed prize Arabians, the best of which belonged to J.W.

The Dukes boarded Arabians for others and had an indoor and outdoor show ring for dressage competitions, auctions and some smaller rodeo events. The Duke Arabians attracted interest from all over the world, and "special visitors" were housed in guesthouses on the property.

He could never give something like this to Laura.

The fancy Arabian barns had their own staff for mucking out stalls and keeping everything spotless, but Cody knew that he'd be expected to fill in as needed. Or maybe not. If it got around that he'd murdered someone, even if they knew it was done to defend his family, it might send the exclusive clientele galloping away faster than their horses.

The thought of gathering a quarter ton of manure this afternoon with a pitchfork and shovel, loading it onto the honey wagon that was attached to a powerful ATV truck and then dumping it bored Cody to no end. He'd rather be training J.W.'s magnificent horses.

Cleaning the stalls was backbreaking work, but he was up for it. Yet he kept looking up at the ranch house, hoping to catch a glimpse of Laura. There was quite a distance from the patio to the remuda barn, but he could spot her anywhere. Laura had a special walk, a kind of bounce in her step, and she always held her head high. Wherever she went, people gravitated to her sunny nature and quick smile. Her eyes sparkled as if she knew a special secret—a good secret—that she was just dying to tell.

But he hadn't seen that Laura yet. She'd appeared briefly at the Double M this afternoon when she'd first seen him, but then that Laura had faded almost immediately.

Obviously, his questions bothered her, but at least she was going to meet him at the creek tonight.

He wanted to find out everything she'd been doing for the past three years, no matter how trivial or insignificant she might think it was. Just the sound of her voice would calm him, might convince him that they'd someday have a chance together again.

And what about the college guy? Did he visit Johnny? Did he take him riding and play with him?

He and Laura had been talking about running away together since high school, but it had been only a hopeful dream. With his mother and Cindy needing him, he couldn't have just up and left.

Georgianna had married Hank Lindy, thinking that they'd all be financially secure forever. His mother assured Cody that Hank would be a good partner for her. He made her laugh. He owned the Duke Springs Tractor and Feed store, and wooed Georgianna with expensive gifts—not jewelry, but farm equipment and feed and grain for the ranch. She was enthralled with Lindy, who had been wonderful and attentive to Cindy…until that fateful night when he stepped over the line and began to knock his mother around until he drew blood.

Then Lindy was going to start with Cindy.

What a beast Lindy had turned out to be, and he'd ruined all their lives.

His and Laura's hopeful dreams had turned into a hopeless mess.

Cody shook off the bad memories and drove the honey wagon to the manure pile, more like a manure *mountain*, and unloaded, then went back to reload.

Slim whistled sharply and motioned for him to hurry. Cody jogged over to him. "What's up?"

"You're supposed to meet with your parole officer and J.W. in J.W.'s office." Slim lit a cigarette and inhaled deeply. "He wants to see you immediately."

Cody had expected a summons sooner or later, but was hoping that it would be later.

"Where?" Cody knew that J.W. had an office at the ranch house. If the meeting was to be there, maybe he could see Laura again.

"In A-2."

Cody forgot that J.W. had another office in the Arabian-2 barn, which was far from the ranch house.

"I'm on my way." Cody hurried away from the smoke of Slim's cigarette and headed down the gravel path leading to A-2.

Cody was in no rush to talk to J.W. or hear about his conditions of parole again from his parole officer. He was instructed on each of them at length before he was released from prison.

He slowed his progress through the desert to J.W.'s office, hoping that his new parole officer would be a decent guy and easygoing. As he walked, he enjoyed the occasional rush of a family of quails in front of him, as well as the dash of a roadrunner.

It was a great day to be free, and it'd be a great night with Laura.

Hawks looped above, black feathery kites against the turquoise sky. He'd like nothing better than to take a long hike through the mountains and connect with the land again. He'd missed being able to do whatever he wanted, whenever he wanted to do it.

Freedom would take some getting used to, but then again, he still was tethered to J. W. Duke.

On the left side of the low, grayish barn,

the door to J.W.'s office was open, but Cody knocked on the door anyway. No one answered, so he paused in the doorway, taking in the scene before him.

J. W. Duke sat in an oversize black leather chair behind a huge, gleaming desk. J.W. was bigger than life and so was his gut. An unlit cigar stub stuck out of the corner of his mouth, and he was shouting into the phone in his usual gruff voice.

J.W. motioned for Cody to take a chair in front of him, but Cody decided to wait outside instead. He couldn't stand breathing in the same air as J.W. any longer than he had to.

"Masters, I'm ready for you!" J.W. bellowed, slamming down the phone.

"I'm here. No need to yell."

"Take a seat." J.W. didn't even glance up at him.

"I'll stand." Cody didn't want to sit in front

of the oak desk as if the other man was his parole officer.

Where was his parole officer anyway?

Although Cody should be grateful for whatever J.W. did to get him out of prison, he didn't want J.W. adding his own spin to his conditions of release.

"Suit yourself, but at least stand where I can see you."

Cody walked to the front of the desk. He liked this vantage point, looking down on J.W. as the man often did to others. The only other man who had always stood toe to toe, belly to belly with J.W. was Mike Masters, Cody's father. The two had had a dislike/respect relationship, if such a thing could exist.

"I thought my parole officer was going to be here," Cody said.

"Something came up. He won't be at our little meeting." J.W. looked him over, then chomped down on his cigar stub. "You got skinnier in jail."

"Not a lot of good food in prison, but I'm sure you didn't bring me here to talk about my diet. Why did you bring me here?"

"What do you mean? Bring you to the Duke Ranch or to my office?"

"Both."

J.W. grunted. "I brought you here to work your ass off and to try and convince you every damn day to sell your sorry ranch to me."

"I figured as much."

"And all you have to do is give me a reason, and I'll send you back to do your other two years with a smile on my face."

Cody grunted. "I figured that, too."

"And no one else is going to give you a job, and you can't leave the county."

Cody shrugged. "Why isn't anyone going to give me a job?" He knew the answer to that, but he wanted to hear it from J.W.

"Because I'll blacklist you, and because you're a murderer."

"I pled to involuntary manslaughter. Not murder."

"I don't care what fancy thing you call it. Your stepfather turned up dead, cowboy."

Cody made as if he was checking his watch, a watch he'd pawned years ago. "Are we almost done here? I have manure that I'd rather shovel."

"I'm not done yet." J.W. took his unlit cigar out of his mouth and set it down on a stack of papers. He pointed his index finger toward Cody's face. "If I catch you near my daughter or my grandson, I'll find a way to send you back. I don't care what I have to do. I have twenty hands who'd swear to whatever I told them to say."

"I'm bound to run into Laura and your grandson. It's a small world, Duke, and I'm working here. What do you want me to do?"

"Run—don't walk—the other way." J.W.

snapped his fingers, then spoke as if he were thinking out loud. "I could always send them both to my sister Betty's in Boston. There's a nice military school nearby for Johnny when he gets older."

Cody remained silent until he said, "All this is about you getting the Double M?"

"Mostly."

"What's the rest of it, Duke?"

"That's *Mr.* Duke to you, *convict.*" The cigar stub returned to his mouth, and he picked up the stack of papers, tapping them on the desk to straighten them. "We're done here. Get back to work."

Outside, the wind had kicked up and so had the dirt, but it was still better than being cooped up with J.W. Cody lowered his hat and bent his head to shield his eyes and nose.

Slim met him in the barn just as he was about to pick up the pitchfork.

"Go home, Cody. You're off the clock."

"What?"

"That's enough for your first day. Hit the trail."

"Thanks, Slim."

"Do me a favor and hurry. I don't want J.W. to see you leaving, so while he's at A-2, take off."

Cody slapped his friend on the back and hurried off to the fence line to cut through to the Double M. He couldn't help looking back at the ranch house to see if there was the usual signal from Laura.

The shade on her right window was open halfway, but she didn't live there anymore. Now, he'd have to look at her cottage for their signal to meet.

Both shades were open. Laura still wanted to meet him tonight at their usual spot.

God help him, he was going to be there.

Laura flinched when she thought of the horrible discussion she'd had with her mother at lunch. Thank goodness Johnny wasn't there to hear what had transpired.

Mike Masters, J. W. Duke, Georgianna and Penny had once been friends who did everything together. Then the page had turned, and the two women soured on each other, then the two men. No. Maybe it was the other way around.

"Mother, that's unkind," Laura had said after her mother's particularly venomous outburst about Georgianna. "You have no right saying things like that about her or anyone else, for that matter. What are you thinking?"

Penny was silent for a while, then snapped, "*No right?* You don't know what you're talking about. I have every right."

"Mother, that's ancient history, for heaven's sake. And you're still not over it?"

"I never will get over it. I loved Mike Masters back then, and Georgianna took him away from me. She said she was pregnant, so he had to marry her. But she wasn't. That was a dirty trick."

Laura sighed. She'd heard this all before, several times.

"But you ended up loving Dad and marrying him."

"But it was still a dirty trick. And Cody is the son of the man who got away."

"And you got stuck with a daughter when you and Dad both wanted a son."

Her mother furrowed her brows. "We love you. That's why we want the best for you, and Cody Masters isn't the one for you."

"Mom, why can't you let me be the judge of that? And why can't you just let the past go? It all worked out, and everyone married who they loved…eventually."

Penny stared in the direction of the Double M. "And then Georgianna went and married that crazy Lindy guy. Too bad she didn't get a dime after Cody killed him."

"Cody didn't do it! I know he didn't."

"So what did he spend three years in prison for? Jaywalking?"

"Mom, I know Cody didn't do anything wrong. He wouldn't hurt a fly." Laura felt a pang of guilt. In her heart of hearts, did she *really* know that?

Penny's fist came down on the table. "Don't you dare try to defend Cody. He was found guilty in court. He went to prison. And as we always told you, you can do better than Cody Masters. And if I find that you've been seeing him, I'm going to file for custody of Johnny due to the fact that your judgment is impaired and that makes you an unfit mother. I don't want Johnny in the company of a murderer."

Stay away from Cody.

Cody will never amount to anything.

He'll never be more than dirt poor, scratching out a living.

She'd heard it numerous times in her life, but that didn't keep her and Cody from becoming friends, then lovers.

But this time, her parents had more ammunition. Cody *was* a murderer.

I'll file for custody of Johnny...unfit mother.

"Don't you dare do such a thing. You couldn't be that cruel."

"I can and I will. And you won't be living here on the ranch anymore."

Laura bit her tongue from screaming at her mother—it wouldn't do any good—but before she changed her mind, she turned and walked away. She didn't want her mother to see her cry. She had to be strong—like a Duke should.

Then she'd regroup and come up with a plan.

This time, the stakes were higher. Laura knew that she shouldn't dare meet Cody, but she couldn't help herself—and she needed to find out the truth from him.

Cody paced by the stream that ran from high in the mountains down to the boundary between the Double M and the Duke ranches.

Now, during the monsoon season, spring to September, it could turn into a raging torrent of water. However, now, during the beautiful month of July, it was reduced to a stream—until the next monsoon.

He took a seat on his usual rock, but kept his flashlight on so he could see Laura approaching and she could see him. He didn't like her having to come out this late at night. She could come face-to-face with coyotes or wolves or any of the nocturnal animals of the desert, any of which could be deadly.

Laura was an Arizona ranch gal, however. She'd carry a gun, especially at night, and had a knife in her boot at all times.

Cody was forbidden to carry a weapon. It was a condition of his parole that he couldn't. He was a convicted felon now, so he'd lost that right. He'd also lost the right to vote and who knew what the hell else.

He smiled, thinking that Laura would have

to protect him. Then he frowned, feeling like half a man for the same reason.

The sound of gravel being scraped snapped him to attention. He stood, almost falling over in his haste.

"Cody?"

"Laura?"

"Yes."

Cody sloshed through the stream in his haste to get her into his arms. She was running, too, and didn't seem to care a whit if her expensive boots got wet and muddy. They embraced in the middle of the water.

"Laura… Laura." He couldn't hold her tight enough.

"I know. I know."

He buried his face in the curve of her neck and inhaled her perfume. He was expecting gardenia, and he wasn't disappointed. It was her scent.

When they kissed, Cody felt as if he'd really come home. Home was Laura.

Their kiss was tentative at first, just a taste, but then he couldn't help himself. He pulled her toward him and when his lips finally touched hers, he released all his frustration, all his loneliness and all his longing for a future with this remarkable woman.

Her straight hair, like spun gold in the moonlight, brushed his arm, and he couldn't stop touching it, threading it through his fingers to enjoy its silkiness.

Cody kissed her forehead, her eyebrows and her neck. Then did it all over again. His hands ran over her back, her shoulders—wherever he could reach without releasing her from his arms, just to make sure she was real.

"You feel so good. Do you still love me, Laura?"

"Of course, Cody. Of course!" She covered

him with kisses, devoured his lips, lifted his T-shirt and ran her hands over his chest.

He was ready and certainly willing to make love to her, but alarms went off in his head. He shouldn't even be here, nor should Laura. To make love with her would be…heaven…but maybe now wasn't a good time.

Cody suspected that there wasn't going to be a good time in their future.

Should he give in to what they both wanted?

Laura stepped back, but held on to his biceps. "I think we need to take things slow. We have to get to know each other again."

His heart took a dive in his chest. "You're right. It's been a long time. And a lot has happened. You got married. You had a son."

"My father has talked to you, hasn't he?" Laura studied his face.

"Yeah."

"He threatened you?"

Cody shrugged. "That doesn't bother me. It's what he can do to you and Johnny."

Her eyes narrowed. "Such as?"

"He could send you away. He said something about your aunt Betty in Boston. He said that there was a nice military school for Johnny there, too."

"I am not going to Boston, and Johnny isn't going to some military school. We are staying right here in our pretty cottage. Besides, this is where you are."

"And I can't leave for at least two years, but I doubt that I can turn around the Double M by then. I don't know if I could ever make it real profitable. We've all tried throughout the years."

Laura moved away from Cody and crossed her arms in front of her chest. It was her turn to pace. "If anyone can turn it around, it's you."

"It takes money, Laura. The place needs an overhaul, and there's none."

"We can never have peace in Duke Springs, Cody. Never. I thought that having a grandchild would mellow them both, and it did to a point, but sometimes it made things worse."

Cody could see the tears swimming in her emerald eyes, and he hugged her to him.

"Oh, that didn't make any sense." She sniffed. "But J.W. would never send us away. He'd miss Johnny too much. My mother had a better threat this morning. She's going to file for custody of Johnny if I consort with a known felon such as you." Cody handed her a red bandanna and she wiped her eyes. "Maybe we ought to stay away from each other. You have too much to lose. So do I."

Cody swore and was just about to punch a saguaro, spikes and all, when Laura closed her hand over his fist and helped him to relax.

"Just tell me, Cody...once and for all, tell me that you are innocent. Tell me that you didn't kill Lindy. Tell me, for heaven's sake."

He pulled his hand away from hers and swore. "I can't. I can't say anything. If I did, all that time I spent in prison would be for nothing."

"Who are you protecting, Cody?"

No answer.

"I need you to tell me, or I can't see you anymore. I might lose my son. Don't you get that?" She was gritting her teeth.

"I didn't kill Lindy!" Cody shouted. "I didn't kill him, but I wish to hell I did." He turned away from her and Laura could tell that he was trying to compose himself. "There, I said it. I finally said it."

She wrapped her arms around him from behind and let her wet cheek rest on his back.

"Who killed him, Cody? Your mother? Cindy? It has to be one of them who did it. You wouldn't go to jail for anyone else."

He turned around and pulled her tight to him. "Please, Laura. That's enough. I shouldn't have even told you what I did. But when you said that your parents—or at least your mother—might try taking Johnny away from you…well, I had to tell you the truth."

"I am so relieved! I mean, I knew you were protecting someone. Why else wouldn't you defend yourself?"

"Please, don't ask me anymore. I can't tell you. If it gets around…"

She kissed him to assure him that he didn't have to speak further. She didn't need to know anything more.

"And I can't sneak around with you forever, Laura. I love you. We've always wanted to get married."

"I know, but can you accept Johnny, too?"

"I admit that I was shocked, and even disappointed, that you slept with someone else, and that you even got married—"

"I never got married, Cody. That was something I just told my parents. They couldn't cope with me having a child out of wedlock. I just told them that I eloped with a fellow student to Vegas so it would make them feel better."

Cody felt the tension slip out of his body. "I'm glad of that. But did you love him? Johnny's father, I mean."

"Yes. I loved him very much, and I know he loved me."

Cody felt sick to his stomach. Why had he even asked that question?

Laura took his hand. "You never answered me. Could you accept Johnny?"

"Of course!" Cody answered almost immediately. "You didn't even have to ask me that. I can't wait to meet him."

"You will—someday."

"And I don't care who the college dude is." Cody couldn't get the picture of Laura sleeping with someone else out of his head. Aw…hell.

"Johnny's the light of my life."

"He should be."

"I don't have any regrets, not one," she said strongly. "Well, maybe one."

"What's that?"

"That Johnny's father doesn't know he's the father of such a wonderful boy."

"He doesn't? Then you should tell him, Laura. A man has the right to know."

"I'll tell him." She remained silent for several heartbeats. "When some important matters get resolved. I don't want Johnny stuck in the middle of a power struggle. Anyway, when the time is right, I'll tell Johnny's father about him."

"When the time is right?" Cody shook his head. "How old did you say Johnny was?"

"He's going to be…uh…four."

"That's a long time to keep a boy from his father."

"I know, Cody. I know. But there are circumstances…"

"Like what?"

Cody had such strong feelings about this. He found it hard to understand why Laura wanted things to stay as they were.

"Let's just drop it. I'll take care of Johnny's father in my own sweet time."

"You've already wasted four years of two lives. If I was a father, I sure as hell would want to know, and would want to participate in raising my child." Cody shook his head. "I don't understand you, Laura."

"Some guys are not like you," Laura shouted, wondering where her anger came from.

"If the college dude doesn't want Johnny, I'll help you raise him. I'll raise him as if he were my own."

"And risk me losing him altogether because you have a criminal record for killing some-one, even though you didn't do it?" A fresh gathering of tears glinted in her eyes, and she closed them and let the tears fall. "It's all such a big mess."

"We can't let anyone take Johnny away from you. We just can't."

She liked how he said "we," but it was really all up to her. She had to handle her parents even more carefully now that Cody was out of prison.

Yes, it was all a big mess, and Laura wondered how to make things neat and tidy.

But that was impossible. They all were headed for a big explosion, and there'd be no turning back.

Chapter Four

Cody took her hand and started down the path that led to the Duke Ranch and her cute little cottage. He must have seen the surprise on Laura's face because he shrugged and said, "What? Do you think I'd let you walk home alone? This entire area is loaded with parolees."

She chuckled. Cody never stayed mad for very long—at least when it concerned her.

"I wish you could come inside and see my home, mine and Johnny's."

"I'd love to, but I don't dare." He sighed. "I was kind of surprised that you weren't staying in the ranch house."

"Johnny and I need our space."

"Good idea."

"But we're up there a lot," Laura explained. "Johnny has a room there for naps and all. Besides, Clarissa and my parents are built-in babysitters when I need them."

She could feel pain radiating from him like a living thing. It was the same pain she felt. They were both trapped in Duke Springs, at least for the next two years.

"J.W. will blackball you from working anywhere around here, even after you are done with parole, unless you sell the Double M to him."

"That's pretty much what I figured out, and that's why, if we have any chance of happiness together, we'll have to move far away from his tentacles. Maybe Washington State or Oregon. Montana. I was even thinking of Canada."

"That's really far. I don't know."

But she did know. No matter how much she loved Cody, she couldn't take Johnny away from her family and friends.

"A picnic," she blurted, stopping in her tracks.

"What?"

"Let's take Johnny on a picnic." It was time for something fun.

"How are we going to pull that off?"

"Easy. This Sunday is the annual church picnic, and I am going to present a check from the Duke Foundation to go toward a new roof and steeple. They are having an old-fashioned box-lunch auction. If you win the auction on my box lunch, you get to have lunch with me."

He shook his head. "You and I having a picnic together? That'll get back to your parents within seconds."

"My parents will be at a horse auction in Gila

Bend. Besides, the box lunch is supposed to be anonymous, but mine will have a red, white and blue ribbon on it. Bid on it, and keep bidding, no matter the cost. I know you haven't gotten paid yet. I'll give you the money."

"I earned some money in prison. Making license plates doesn't pay as well as it did before, but I have twenty-three whole bucks, so don't worry about it." He was joking, but it saddened Laura to think of him inside doing that instead of working with horses and being on the Double M.

He dropped her hand and stuffed his into the pocket of his jeans. "Laura, it's not going to work."

"Of course it will. If my parents find out, I'll just explain that there was no way you knew that box was mine, and that I had to have lunch with you due to the rules of the auction."

"Sweetheart, I can't go to the picnic. I'll get the big snub from the good folks of the church.

I don't think you're ready for that, and I don't want to subject Johnny to any talk about his mother being with a killer."

Laura looked deep into Cody's eyes. By the light of the full moon, she could see the pain in them. "I've thought about that, Cody. But these people are your friends. A lot of them stood by you in court."

"A lot of them wanted my head on a platter," he snapped.

She took his hand. "We'll go off on our own to have lunch—me, you and Johnny. I don't care about people talking about us, but if we're far enough away from people when we have our picnic, Johnny won't hear anything."

"I don't know, Laura."

"Let's try it, Cody. You have to go out in public sooner or later."

"I was hoping that it'd be later, but okay."

"See you Sunday, then?" she asked.

"Sunday."

She leaned forward, resting her head on his chest. "Two days." Stepping back, she ran her palms down his cheeks to see if he was real and to make sure that this wasn't a dream. Taking his face in her hands, she pulled him toward her for a kiss—a long, sensuous kiss—full of longing, hope and a wish for a quick solution to all of their problems.

Finally, it was Sunday, the day of the church picnic. Cody did enough work at both ranches to merit a long soak in the creek.

So he sat in his favorite spot with his back against a rock letting the cool water rush around him, thinking.

It felt strange to just relax and have an unstructured day. He still hadn't shaken off the institutional mentality of schedules and timetables, and caught himself checking for a clock on numerous occasions, thinking that it was time for his cell block to line up for lunch or shower time, or for an academic or training program.

He couldn't wait to see Laura again and meet her son. He wondered if he could see Laura's face in the little boy, or if he looked like the college guy. He wondered about Johnny's personality and what the little boy liked to eat and watch on TV. He didn't know what cartoons, which were a big favorite of the inmates, or shows were out these days. Instead of TV, Cody kept busy reading and doing work for his bachelor's degree, which was how he got the nickname Professor.

His graduation at the prison was a small affair—about a dozen inmates and a handful of dignitaries from both the University of Arizona and the prison. Following that, there was a little reception in the prison library with punch and cake.

So now he had a bachelor's degree in American history because animal husbandry wasn't offered. Not that he'd be able to do much with an American history degree—no one would ever hire him to teach in their school—but he'd always loved history and because school passed the time.

He'd have to tell Laura someday. She'd like that he got a degree. J.W. wouldn't give a damn—it wasn't a degree in business or finance or ranch management. Cody decided to keep his mouth shut. J.W. took too much pleasure in employing ranch hands with degrees who couldn't find jobs in their academic fields, and Cody didn't want to give him any more reasons to be amused at his expense.

Cody pushed away all thoughts of J.W. He planned on having a great day at the church picnic.

He hauled himself out of the water, sloshed to the bank of the creek and wiped himself dry with his T-shirt. In the Arizona heat, his jeans would dry before he hiked back to the Double M.

He'd take a decent shower then. He couldn't get enough of long, hot showers.

Draping his shirt around his neck, he slid into his cowboy boots and began walking. He could walk the way in his sleep, and so could Laura. He wondered why no one had discovered this part of the creek—although he doubted that J.W. and Penny would step a toe in it, since it was on Masters land. By the time it meandered to Duke property, it was nothing more than a muddy trickle.

The creek would come with the Double M, if his mother ever decided to give up the fight.

Although he'd like to think that it was his blood, sweat and tears that made the Double M what it was, his mother was the one who had kept it going for the three years that he was gone and just after his father died.

After Mike Masters died of cancer, Cody fell

apart. He'd started drinking heavily, hitting the sleazy bars in the next county that didn't care about his age and missed more school than he attended. When he was physically in the classroom, his mind was elsewhere.

It was Laura Duke who'd picked him up, dusted him off and then told him off. With a lot of hard work, he caught up so he could graduate with the rest of his class.

He jogged the short distance to the ranch. His mother was pushing a wheelbarrow full of dirty straw, heading for the manure pile.

Cindy was weeding the vegetable garden. He grinned when she waved her pink, flowered gardening gloves at him.

Then she screamed, not moving from her kneeling position.

Both Cody and his mother came running.

"S-snake," she said quietly, pointing a finger to the right of her. "Rattler."

Cody felt for the Colt at his side. He usually

carried a gun for protection from snakes and other wild animals that might get a jump on him, the horses or cattle.

But there was no gun at his side. Dammit! Now what?

"Cindy, stay perfectly still. Don't move," Cody said evenly, softly.

"I don't want to get bit. I got bit before and it hurt. Hospital."

"Don't move. Don't cry. Don't panic." Cody looked around to find something—anything— to use. He was so out of practice, he doubted that he could hit the snake with a rock.

His mother handed him the pitchfork that she had nearby. He'd never be able to toss that and hit the snake. Besides, he didn't want to hurt Cindy.

"Mom, I need a gun. Or a knife."

He wasn't bad at throwing knives. He used to practice constantly with a target taped to a hay bale.

"Wait," his mother said, walking backward toward the barn. Then at a comfortable distance away from Cindy and the snake, she turned and ran into it.

"You'll be okay, Cindy," Cody said. "I'll take care of Mr. Snake."

"Hurry up! Please, Cody. Please."

"Don't move, sweetie," his mother said, returning from the barn. "Cody's going to get it."

His mother handed him his father's old .22. Cody hesitated, remembering one of the conditions of parole—he wasn't supposed to possess or use a firearm.

"It's shaking its rattler at me!" Cindy said through gritted teeth. "Its mouth is open. I see his teeth." She was crying now.

Cody eyed the nearby pitchfork and looked for a rock he could throw. Neither would work at his distance.

He had to help his sister. She was bitten before and had a terrible reaction. She was in the hospital for days.

"Cody, please take the shot. You're the only one who can make it," his mother said.

He took the gun from his mother and focused on the snake. He'd have to shoot right into the sun. He took a long, deep breath and was about to squeeze the trigger when he chickened out.

"You can do it," his mother said softly, evenly. "You have good aim, Cody. Your father taught you."

"It's been a long time, Mom."

"It's like riding a bike, isn't it?"

Her statement was so ludicrous that it made the knot between his shoulders disappear. He took careful aim, let out his breath and fired.

He missed!

Just as the thing was about to strike, he emptied the gun and didn't stop until the snake was in pieces.

Cindy came running over and launched herself into his arms. "Thank you!"

Turning, she hugged her mother. "I was so scared. I should be used to snakes by now."

Georgianna rubbed her daughter's back. "Cindy, I hate snakes, too. Always have, always will. And I'll never get used to them, so don't worry."

Just then, a grayish-blue Prius came down their driveway in a whirlwind of dust. The three of them watched the vehicle approach, trying to guess who it might be.

"Got any idea who that is, Mom?" Cody asked.

"No idea."

"Cindy, how about you? Any idea?"

"Nope."

A man in a suit got out of the car. His pants were too short and his crocodile boots were too new. He held a small, three-ring binder in his hand and glanced at it.

"Hello. You must be Cody Masters."

"I must be."

"I'm Leland Charles, your parole officer."

Officer Charles suddenly skidded to a stop, then turned and ran toward his Prius. He was a portly guy and ran like a penguin. He opened the door and squatted behind it.

Dammit! He was pointing a gun at them. His hands were shaking and his face was flaming red.

"What the hell?" Cody lifted his hands up in surrender, finally realizing that he still held on to his father's gun.

"Wait. Mr…uh…" He drew a blank. What the hell was his parole officer's name?

"Leland Charles," Cindy supplied.

"Mr. Charles, please. It's not what you think."

"Put your gun down, Masters! Immediately!" Officer Charles ordered. "Kneel down on the ground. Hands behind your head!"

"There's been a misunderstanding," Cody said.

"Yeah, and you made it, Masters."

Cindy burst into tears. "Sir, I didn't want to get bit. There was a snake in the garden."

His mother stepped forward. "That's absolutely true, Officer Charles. I gave him the gun. No one could have made that shot except Cody."

"Step back from the parolee, please."

"C'mon, Cindy, wipe your eyes and stand by Mom. We'll get this straightened out," Cody said.

Cody carefully set the gun down on the dirt, barrel facing away from everyone. He held his hands up so Officer Charles could see he was unarmed. Then he knelt down, hands behind his head, feeling every bit the criminal.

"Don't you dare even breathe, Masters," Officer Charles shouted, stepping away from behind his car door and slamming it shut. His gun never wavered from Cody.

"Holding my breath, Parole Officer Charles. Holding breath!" Cody shouted, just as he was trained to do in prison.

He heard the snap of a leather case, then the sound of metal handcuffs being fumbled, then felt them clamp around one wrist than the other.

Officer Charles picked up the .22 from the ground and checked the chambers. "Empty," Charles said.

"I know," Cody said, shifting his knees on the gravel. "I used every bullet on the snake. I'm a little rusty."

Charles tucked the .22 into the back of his pants and unceremoniously hauled Cody to his feet.

"You're in violation of your parole conditions, Masters."

"I know, but it couldn't be helped. I needed to protect my sister."

"Officer Charles, can we talk for a moment? I'm sure we can clear this up," Georgianna asked quietly.

Cindy walked toward them and stood at Cody's side. "Sir, I told you that my brother killed a rattlesnake that was going to bite me."

"And I handed him the gun. It was in the barn," Georgianna said again, standing almost toe to toe with Officer Charles. "Only Cody could have made that shot. I can show you the snake, if you'll follow me."

Cindy made a funny sound in her throat. "Cody wasn't going to shoot you. He'd never do that."

Officer Charles grunted. "He certainly would do that, young lady. Why do you think he went to jail in the first place?"

"Oh. But he—" Cindy looked at her mother, and Cody could see that things were going to get worse pretty soon if he didn't do something, and fast.

"Officer Charles, could we talk in private?" Cody motioned with his head to a shady spot on the front porch. "With a side trip to the garden first?"

Charles put a hand on the link of his cuffs. "Walk."

Cody was thankful that the man didn't lift his cuffed hands up as some law enforcement types just had to do to show power. It hurt his shoulders. But Charles didn't seem to be that type.

"Over there," Cody said. "By the peppers."

"Jalapeños?" he asked.

"Yeah."

Officer Charles bent over and looked at the ground. "Looks like it was a rattler once."

"And now?"

"Now it looks likes mincemeat."

"I'm a little out of practice," Cody said.

"Let's keep it that way."

"Look, Officer Charles, I'd never shoot you, for heaven's sake. I'm not going to shoot anyone unless they are harming someone I love."

"Was Hank Lindy hurting someone you love?"

"You have my file. You must have read it," Cody said. "Now, can you get me out of these cuffs? I don't want my mother and sister to see me like this much longer."

His parole officer thought for a while, then finally said, "I have to take you downtown. We'll have a meeting with my supervisor. You can tell him your story."

"Will you remove the handcuffs?"

"Not till we meet with my boss."

"Would you like to go on the porch and talk? It's damn hot out here. Maybe my mother will get us something cold to drink." He turned to her, and she nodded, hurrying into the house with Cindy.

"Yeah. I think we still need to talk."

Cody led the way to the porch. Officer Charles sat down with a grunt and loosened his tie. "You gave me quite a scare, Masters."

Cody grinned and sat, leaning forward so the cuffs wouldn't dig into his wrists. "Same here, Parole Officer Charles."

Cody finally got a chance to look at the man. He looked pretty solid, but had a beer belly, probably due to his desk job. He had brown hair, cut into a brush cut, and was probably ex-military. His face was average-looking, except for his nose. That had been broken at one time, maybe more. He had some laugh lines around his mouth and the corners of his eyes, and Cody hoped that the man was fair, not a puppet of J. W. Duke's.

Actually, Cody had warmed to Officer Charles immediately for being nice to his mother and sister.

"I am formally informing you that you're in

violation of your parole for having a firearm in your possession and for using it," he said.

"If you want to get technical, you're right. But isn't there any room for special circumstances?" Cody held his breath. If he had to go back to jail now that he'd had a taste of freedom, he'd fall apart.

"It's my job to be technical. In retrospect, would you do it again?"

"Shoot the snake to protect my little sister?" Cody asked, making sure that they were both on the same page and that Charles wasn't asking about the incident that got him to prison in the first place.

Officer Charles hesitated. "Yeah, the gun. Would you do it again?"

"Absolutely. I wouldn't hesitate a bit. No matter how many parole conditions I violated. She couldn't handle being bitten again. She was bitten before and landed in the hospital for just short of a week."

"Okay."

"Okay, what, sir? Should I go inside and get my toothbrush?"

"Nah. You know that they'll give you a brand-new one at the Arizona State big house."

Cody knew that Officer Charles was joking, but his heart sank as he just thought about going back. It felt as if he was going to barf. He couldn't go back there, he just couldn't. His mother needed him. His sister needed him. And he'd like to think that Laura and her son needed him. Just when they were connecting again, he wouldn't see her for two more years.

This gun thing was bogus. He didn't want to feel sorry for himself, but how much more could he take?

Johnny. He wanted to get to know Laura's son.

Cody wanted to put a fist through the wall of the ranch house, but it would probably fall apart.

He could hear his mother and Cindy sobbing from inside the house.

Officer Charles inclined his head toward the house. He could hear them crying, too. "I know there was a snake, Cody, and that you greeting me with a gun in your hand was coincidental."

"It was, sir."

"I'll tell you what, Masters. I'll call my supervisor from here. I'll discuss the matter with her, and we'll decide if I'm going to file a violation of parole against you and take you downtown." He got up from his chair, stood by his car and punched in some numbers on his cell.

As Cody watched Officer Charles on the phone, he said every prayer he knew. Then he remembered that he had a date with Laura at the church picnic.

It looked like he wasn't going to make it.

Chapter Five

Laura scanned the crowd for Cody, but she didn't see him. Soon, church officials escorted her to the makeshift stage in front of the band that was tuning up, and sat her down in one of a long line of folding chairs.

Johnny sat next to her, a perfect little gentleman, at least for now. He seemed to sense that he had to behave because something important was going to happen. Laura smiled when she remembered Johnny asking her if he could wear a suit and tie "like Grandpa." Grandpa

wore a suit only when he went to horse or cattle auctions.

So, she went to the only clothing store in
town—the one now owned by Hank Lindy's
son, Steven—to get Johnny a suit, dress shirt
and new, longer tie for the boy since he'd grown
taller. Only in Duke Springs would there be a
combination feed, clothing and hardware store.

Laura wondered why Georgianna Masters
Lindy didn't get the store in Lindy's will, since
she was married to Hank at the time of his
death. If Georgianna knew the answer to that,
she was keeping it quiet. Maybe it was because
his son, Steve, had worked at the store forever.
He was the natural successor to his father.

Laura put her hand on Johnny's knee to stop
him from swinging his feet. The program had
better start soon. Laura dropped off her meal
with the red, white and blue ribbon to the box-
lunch committee at the designated table, hop-

ing that Cody would remember to bid on that one, no matter what the cost.

Where was Cody?

Finally, the bidding was about to start. Reverend Pangburn welcomed the crowd to the picnic, stating that he hoped everyone would have a good time and that he was looking forward to being the auctioneer for the boxed lunches.

Two more parishioners spoke about upcoming events. Finally, it was Laura's turn. She took Johnny's hand and stepped up to the podium. Someone gave Johnny a chair to stand on and helped him get up. Laura put an arm around Johnny to steady him, but instead of beginning her speech, she checked the crowd for Cody one more time.

He still wasn't here.

She smiled at the people, nodded at Reverend Pangburn and the rest of the dignitaries, and took a deep breath.

"I will keep this short because I know that

you can't wait to start the festivities. So, on be-half of the Duke Foundation, I'd like to present Reverend Pangburn with a check for the repair of the church's roof and steeple." She paused for the round of applause and cheers that came from the audience. "I'd also like to add that any profit realized today from the carnival will be matched by the Duke Foundation."

There were more cheers and applause.

Other than investing the foundation's money and playing the stock market to refurbish the funds, this was the best part of her job: giving away her father's money to causes that mat-tered. Matter of fact, this was the second roof she'd funded. The first one was the Double M's.

If J.W. ever found that out, he'd have a fit, and she'd be out of a job, and she loved her job.

After the ceremony, she and Johnny walked the grounds, stopping to play the games spe-cifically designed for children. Johnny won several stuffed animals and other prizes and couldn't be happier.

"Momma, can I have some blue cotton candy?"

"Not until after lunch. We have to eat lunch first."

And it looked as if they'd be eating alone.

She pulled out her cell phone to call Cody, but she couldn't. He didn't have a cell phone.

But this wasn't like Cody. Unless something was wrong, he would have found a phone and called her.

She looked at her phone, willing it to ring. She should just call Georgianna, for heaven's sake, but she didn't want to alarm her or Cindy if Cody was just running late.

Over the loudspeaker came the announcement that the box-lunch auction was starting. Disappointment washed over her like a tidal wave. She was so looking forward to this time with Cody and Johnny—just the three of them.

The man she'd always loved...and their son!
Finally, Reverend Pangburn held up the first box decorated with flowers and feathers. There was good-natured heckling as husbands bid against husbands—even the women got into the act.

Then Reverend Pangburn held up her box. "This is a beautiful box lunch, very patriotic. And on the note it says that it's fried chicken, apple pie and potato salad."

"I bid fifteen dollars," said a man with bib overalls that Laura didn't recognize.

"Twenty bucks," said George Coleman, one of the deacons in the church who was always after her for a date.

"Thirty dollars," said a voice in the crowd. It was the choir director, Louise LaClare. She was just driving the price up.

"Fifty dollars!"

There was a big "oh" that went up from the

crowd, then applause. Heads swiveled to see the big bidder.

Laura's head swiveled the most. Then she saw him. Cody. He was leaning against a wooden railed fence. Only those who knew him closely would know that his nonchalant stance was hiding a man who was coiled and ready to spring.

"Fifty dollars from Cody Masters," said Reverend Pangburn, who'd been one of Cody's supporters when he was first arrested. "Welcome back, Cody. It's good to see you."

Cody tweaked the brim of his hat to the reverend and nodded.

Most of the faithful parishioners smiled and nodded back to Cody. The rest murmured among themselves, pointing at him.

"Fifty dollars going once," said Reverend Pangburn. "Fifty dollars twice. Sold to Cody Masters. One picnic lunch. Whoever packed this beautiful basket, please pick it up and take it over to Cody to join him."

Laura's heart pounded as she felt everyone's eyes on her and Johnny. She took her son's hand and approached the stage to claim her boxed lunch.

Reverend Pangburn covered his microphone and leaned over to talk to her. "If you don't want to have lunch with Cody Masters, I'll certainly understand. We can work something else out."

"Why wouldn't I want to have lunch with Cody?" she asked.

"Well, he just got out of jail and some women would shy away from a criminal—a murderer."

"Then those women aren't very Christian, are they, Reverend Pangburn? He's paid his debt to society—no, he's still paying. Besides, I've known Cody for all my life, and so has most everyone at this event."

Laura took her picnic basket, and with Johnny in tow, they walked over to Cody.

"Cody Masters, I'd like you to meet my son, Johnny Duke. Johnny, this is Mr. Masters."

"Hi," Johnny said, studying Cody.

"Howdy, partner."

Johnny was the cutest little guy that he'd ever seen. He was trying to look so grown-up and important in his little suit. Johnny had dark blond hair, the most striking blue eyes and a little dimple on the right side of his mouth.

Cody could see the resemblance to Laura, although Laura didn't have dimples. Cody's sister, Cindy, had them and he thought they looked as cute as hell whenever she laughed or smiled.

Cody squatted down to be somewhat level with Johnny's eyes. "Johnny, you're looking mighty fine for our picnic with your suit on."

Cody looked down at his own chambray shirt

and well-worn jeans. His shirtsleeves were rolled up and showed sunburned arms that were finally turning tan. He wore a shiny belt buckle that he'd won at some rodeo competition. He had so many buckles and prizes, that he should try to sell them for extra money to put into the Double M. His boots were scuffed and dirty after delivering the snake pieces into the desert. "I'm looking like a bum compared to you, Johnny."

Cody held his hand out, and Johnny shook it. Then they bumped knuckles, which turned into a high five.

Johnny nodded very seriously. "Momma said that this was an important day. My grandpa wears this when it's important."

"It's an important day, Johnny?" Cody asked. "Because of the picnic?"

"No. It's because we gave the church money," Johnny said. "We're really rich, you know."

Laura winced. "Did Grandpa J.W. tell you that?"

Johnny nodded. "We have to show people how nice we are so they won't be jealous of our money."

Cody was amused. "Maybe you shouldn't talk about how rich you are, and just be nice to everyone. You think?"

The little guy thought about it for a while as he dug the toe of a polished shoe into the desert sand. "Okay." He lifted his little shoulders. "I'm hungry now. Are you going to eat with us, Cody?"

"That's Mr. Masters," Laura corrected.

"Mr. Masters, are you going to eat with us?"

"If your mother will let me."

"She has to. You bought her basket. It's the rule." He tugged on Laura's arm. "Let's eat, Momma."

Laura chuckled. "Let's picnic by the creek. There's a nice spot up there."

"Sounds good," Cody said, taking the picnic basket from her hand. "Johnny, will you let me hold your hand?"

"I guess so."

When Johnny slipped his little hand into his, Cody fell in love. This boy could have been his.

"Cody, you were late. Is everything okay?"

He grinned and let out a deep breath. "Yes, it all worked out in the end. I'm fine. Really fine. I'll tell you about it later."

She raised an eyebrow. "Okay."

Cody bit his lip from asking Laura the question that had been boring into his brain since he found out Laura had a son: why hadn't she waited for him? They'd had plans. Cody was going to make his mark in the world and show J.W. that he was finally good enough for Laura.

J.W. had told him many times that he was not right for his daughter. Deep inside, in his heart of hearts, he knew that he could never marry Laura now. Now he was a jailbird, a killer, despite all his best intentions. But even if he could turn back the hands of time, he'd still do the same thing. He'd go to court, plead guilty and do his time.

Then it hit him. He was a jailbird lunching with a sweet little impressionable boy and a woman from the leading family in Duke Springs.

I shouldn't have come here. I should leave now.

Heaven help him, he wanted to stay. He wanted to be with Laura and get to know her son. He wanted to have lunch with them.

Didn't he deserve some happiness? Just for a while?

Laura almost cried when she saw Johnny's little hand in Cody's big, work-rough hand. She could tell by Cody's bright eyes and big grin that he'd already fallen in love with his son.

Laura's heart warmed and broke in half at the same time.

Why did I bring the two of them together? Cody would soon realize that Johnny was his son.

She tried to tamp down her conflicted feelings and vowed to relax and have a good time at the picnic. She desperately needed a break from worrying.

Laura spread a red-checkered tablecloth on the ground and they all sat down. Then she unpacked plates, forks, napkins and a plastic jug of iced tea and cups.

"We have potato salad, fried chicken and apple pie," she said. "I made everything but the fried chicken. Clarissa made that." Laura helped Johnny out of his suit coat.

"You could take your tie off, Johnny," Laura suggested.

"I don't want to."

"Okay." She began to make a plate for him.

"Everything looks delicious," Cody said. "A real feast."

"Hey, Cody, did you go to jail?" Johnny asked.

Cody almost choked on his iced tea.

"Johnny, that's not a nice thing to ask anyone," Laura tucked a napkin under his chin. "Where did you hear that?"

He turned to his mother and said, "I heard Grandpa say it." Then he looked at Cody. His eyes were wide in awe. "Was it cool there?"

"Cool?"

Laura could tell that Cody was just about to spew the granddaddy of all swearwords, but he realized that he wasn't in cell block 16. He was sitting by the sluggish creek on the church's grounds with her and Johnny, who was obviously enthralled with the whole jail thing.

Cody looked as if he was trying to find the right words. "No, Johnny, it wasn't cool at all. It was plain awful."

"Johnny, eat your chicken. Don't ask Mr. Masters about such a thing. Let's enjoy our lunch."

"But Mom—"

She fixed a napkin over his shirt. "No buts."

"Laura, if you don't mind, I'd like to answer Johnny's questions."

"Are you sure you don't mind?"

"Not a bit."

She trusted Cody not to go into detail, and to let Johnny know that jail wasn't "cool." "Go ahead."

The brightness left Cody's face, as if a dark cloud decided to float in front of him.

"I never had a nice picnic like this in jail. Never."

"No picnics?" Johnny stopped eating and was as still as a statue.

"None. And there's no delicious food like your mom and grandma and Clarissa make. And you can't just walk anywhere you want. And there are no ponies in jail."

"No Pirate?" Johnny's mouth fell open.

"No Pirate. Slim would have to take care of Pirate. Or your mother. Someone would have to ride him, too, if you're not around."

"I wanna ride Pirate. He's my pony."

Cody shook his head. "See how jail's not cool, son?"

Laura's heart pounded in her chest, and her face felt as if it was on fire. Cody had called Johnny "son."

She took a couple of deep breaths and told herself that it was just a term that everyone used to address a young kid.

It was no big deal.

It meant nothing.

"Jail isn't cool," Johnny said. "Can I have a soda?"

"*May* I have a soda?" Laura corrected.

"That's what I said, Momma! I want a soda."

Cody chuckled and Laura shot him a stern look with a slight smile so Johnny couldn't see. He turned his head, but she could still see Cody's shoulders shaking with silent laughter.

"Johnny, how about iced tea instead of soda?" Laura asked.

"Well, okay," Johnny said.

Laura stole a glance at Cody as she poured more iced tea for Johnny. He was lying on his back, looking up at the sky. His smile had disappeared and there was tightness around his mouth.

He was remembering something about his time in prison. She wanted to take his hand, but not when there were other people picnicking along the creek and could see them. Someone would certainly take exception, and word would get back to J.W.

It was going to be bad enough when J.W. and Penny found out about their picnic together, but she just couldn't be seen holding Cody's hand.

"Would you like some chicken, Cody?" she asked.

"Sure would."

She passed him the container. As she'd hoped, their hands touched under the plastic bowl and lingered there.

"Thank you," she whispered. "You did a great job answering Johnny. That couldn't have been easy for you."

"It's okay. He's a great kid, Laura," Cody whispered back. "Smart, and as cute as can be."

Laura grinned. "And he's almost four, going on forty."

"I thought you said he's already four."

"That's what I meant."

Right now the little cowboy was singing to himself and swinging the drumstick as if he was a conductor.

"I'm done eating, Momma. Can I have some pie?"

"Not yet. Wait until after we eat the main course, sweetie."

Laura pulled some small, metal trucks and cars out of her purse. "Wipe your hands and mouth and play with your cars for a while."

"Okay."

Laura and Cody ate in comfortable silence until Cody started playing cars with Johnny. She watched them, enjoying her two favorite guys interacting. Cody was a natural with kids.

Would Cody notice that Johnny had his eyes—eyes that were as blue as turquoise? How about the tiny little dimple on the right side of the boy's mouth? It peeked out when Johnny was smiling, just like Cody's did, although Cody always denied he had a dimple.

Johnny's hair wouldn't give him a hint. It was a gold-blond, just like hers.

She'd thought she'd have a plan by now to introduce Cody to his son, but with J.W. and her mother's attitude toward Cody, she didn't want to do or say anything that might return him to jail.

If she told Cody that he was Johnny's father, Cody would want to be a major presence in Johnny's life, and J.W. would fight him at every turn.

Cody would push her into marrying him, and have Johnny and her move into the Double M. That would be the only place in which they could live.

Georgianna would accept them with open arms.

Cindy would be delighted.

But it would mean the fast track to jail for Cody. Somehow, J.W. would see to it that he'd be out of the way, and out of her and Johnny's lives.

She was walking on glass shards, trying not to get cut.

J.W. and Penny would hire a team of the best family court lawyers in the country. Sure, her father loved Johnny, but also he wanted a male heir to take over the Duke Ranch, and, of course, Johnny was in training to do so.

J.W. knew that she was longing to run things, but unfortunately her father thought that because she was born female, she didn't know a thing about running a ranch and never would. But J.W. was willing to wait for a decade or so until Johnny was ready.

However, if Johnny wasn't interested and wanted to pursue another career path, J.W. would fall apart. Then what?

Laura sighed. If Johnny wanted to do something else, then Laura would see to it and let the chips fall where they may.

Everyone has a right to be happy, don't I? Oops... I mean, didn't they?

Chapter Six

Cody helped himself to another plate of chicken and potato salad and ate as if he was on death row and it was his last meal. Johnny was playing catch with another little boy about his age.

"I thought you weren't coming today," Laura said.

"I almost didn't."

"What happened? Slim wouldn't let you out of work?"

"Slim's pretty fair, but that's not it." Cody

scooped more potato salad onto his fork. "My parole officer thought that I was going to shoot him."

"What?"

"I'll explain," Cody said.

"You're going to have to."

Laura held her breath and listened intently as he did just that. "What a close call, Cody. He might have shot you."

"I never thought that killing a snake would cause such a ruckus. Bad timing on the snake's part and mine, I guess."

"You weren't carrying the gun, were you?" Laura asked. She could barely get out the words, her mouth was so dry. She reached for her iced tea and took several cool swallows.

"No. My mother got it. She knew I could kill the snake, even as rusty as I am."

"Seems like you weren't all that rusty. You saved Cindy from getting bitten," Laura said.

Another reason why she couldn't let Cody

into Johnny's life was that he could be yanked away at any time and returned to jail to do his last two years.

It'd be just awful for Laura to wait two more years for Cody, but it would seem like forever to a little boy. She couldn't let Johnny get close to Cody. If he went away, it would hurt the little boy.

Darn it! She just didn't know what to do.

She should tell Cody that Johnny was his. He'd missed out on enough of Johnny's life, but it would just open a can of worms that she didn't know how to contain yet.

Sooner or later, Cody would figure out that he was the guy she'd had a one-night stand with in college. Yes, he was the "college guy" she'd made love to on one very fertile night when he was helping her move into the dorm.

She could see Cody staring at Johnny, looking him over. Thinking…wondering…doing the math. She could just tell Cody before he asked her.

So far, the college-guy story had worked on Georgianna and Cindy, as well as her parents. She hoped that it'd work on Cody for a while until she could sort out this big mess.

Until then, she had to keep Johnny away from Cody, she decided.

Just let them enjoy this one picnic together.

She smiled as she watched Cody, Johnny and Johnny's new friend playing catch. Cody was lobbing the ball to them, and they'd throw it back with all their might. Cody caught their pitches, although he had to work for most of them, due to some wild throws.

The three of them were doing some good-natured teasing as they tossed the ball.

Then everything changed.

"Danny! Daniel Stevenson, get back here im-mediately." She and Cody heard the loud shriek coming from a woman standing with her hands on her hips. "Get back here!"

Danny must have been Johnny's little friend, because he stopped playing. He shook his head. "I'm playing catch."

The woman stomped over, grabbing Danny's hand and half dragged him away. He started to cry. "Why do I have to go? I want to play with Johnny and Cody."

"You are not to go near Cody Masters!" his mother yelled.

Laura stood up. She remembered Liz Stevenson now. She was a vocal member of the church, but hadn't seemed to grasp the idea of charity and tolerance to her fellow man.

Cody waved Laura back. "Let it go."

The picnickers dotting the lawn and sitting along the creek craned their necks or stood to see what was happening.

Laura didn't want Johnny to be part of some

kind of scene that was transpiring, so she motioned to him to come to the blanket.

"I wanna stay and play catch. I like Cody. He's teaching me how to pitch," Danny yelled.

Laura turned to Johnny. "Stay here, sweetie." She walked past Cody. Just as he saw her, he held out his arm to stop her.

"Skip it, Laura. It's not worth it."

She wasn't going to listen to Cody and stay put. If he wasn't going to stick up for himself, she'd stick up for him. She jogged over to Liz Stevenson and Danny.

"Mrs. Stevenson, what seems to be the problem?"

"You darn well know, Laura Duke. I don't want my Danny exposed to a criminal." She lowered her voice to a whisper. "A murderer."

"Cody Masters won my basket." Laura tried to be as polite as possible. "And he did his time, and Danny's having a good time playing catch. I've been watching, and Cody has taught both boys a lot. Don't take Danny away from having fun."

"Danny, go sit down on our blanket. Now, where's your dad? Oh, he's over there."

Danny's father was having a beer with a couple of other men at a picnic table. He wasn't paying any attention to his son at what was a family event.

She raised an eyebrow. "Mrs. Stevenson, Cody Masters is a good man. Let Danny play with Johnny and him."

"He's a criminal, pure and simple. I'm just surprised that your father and mother aren't objecting...or don't they know?"

She was so loud, as if she was preaching to the crowd without a microphone.

"As I told you, Cody won the bid on my picnic basket, so we are eating together. That's all."

Laura bit her lip, feeling like a fraud. She was no better than Liz Stevenson because she was lying to Cody about Johnny's paternity. Because she was ashamed about his label as a murderer and afraid that she'd lose her son.

"That's all? Who are you kidding? I wasn't born yesterday, Laura. You and Cody Masters have been sneaking around for years."

"Mrs. Stevenson, our conversation is over."

"I never wanted it to start in the first place."

Oh, that was a major slam, and that didn't sit well with Laura. She was going to get in the last word no matter what.

"You are so narrow-minded, I can't reach you," she said, then turned and walked back to Cody, who was sitting cross-legged with Johnny.

"Cody, I'll cut us some pie now."

"No, thanks, Laura. I've lost my appetite."

Johnny sat for a while, eating a slice of apple pie. Then he went over to the edge of the shallow creek and was shooting stones into it.

"Cody, are you going to let a nutcase like Liz Stevenson bother you?" Laura said. "Then you're not the man I thought you were."

"She's right, you know. I am a criminal. A killer. Even if I did it to defend my family, I will always be a murderer. Kids shouldn't be hanging around me, and vice versa."

He was only playing catch, but he loved being with the boys.

Just when he'd been having such a great time. He hated to be reminded about his past. Well, it had only been his past since about three days ago.

"I should really get back to work," he said.

"It's Sunday," Laura pointed out.

"I'm talking about the Double M. It's my one day off from your place."

"I see." Laura nodded. "And you want to get out of here. Right?"

"You know it."

"It'll look like you're running scared, Cody,

and the Cody I know never runs from anything. Is that what you want?"

She was right. He was so beaten down by his stint in the can that it was hard to remember the man he used to be.

But the man he used to be should have eloped with Laura after their high school graduation.

They would have made it somehow.

But now he couldn't leave the Double M or his mother and little sister, and he couldn't leave Laura—or even Johnny. The boy was the cutest, and Cody loved him already because he was Laura's.

Was he the college guy? Was he the one that she'd made love with and gotten her pregnant with Johnny? He was her first, he knew that.

No, absolutely not. He couldn't be the boy's father. He dismissed the thought.

For sure, Laura would have told him.

"Johnny," Cody shouted. "Would you like to toss the ball around again?"

"Sure!"

Laura packed everything away, then watched them for a while.

"What do you want to be when you get older, Johnny?" Cody asked.

"A rancher, just like my grandpa. I want to have a lot of horses like he has, and I'll ride Pirate whenever I want, and I'll have cows, too, but I only want chocolate cows."

"Chocolate cows?"

"For chocolate milk." Johnny laughed.

"Oh." Cody chuckled. He fell for that old chestnut.

"I wanna give away money like my momma, too."

"That's a noble profession," Cody said.

"Huh?"

"That's a nice thing to do. I'm sure your mother likes doing that."

"She said that it makes her feel good."

He'd feel good giving away J.W.'s money, too.

"She gave away a roof to Mrs. Georgie next door. And Cindy. I call her Cindy Lou Who. She's my friend."

"Whoa. She gave away a roof?" Cody paused. "How do you know that, Johnny?"

He shrugged.

"Oh, I'm going to have to be more careful around little children with big ears," Laura said.

"Mrs. Georgie's roof was falling down. What if she got wet? What if Cindy and Mrs. Georgie got hurt?" He shook his head solemnly.

He looked over at Laura. Her eyes were as wide as one of his gold belt buckles and her mouth was pinched tight.

So J. W. Duke's money had funded the Double M's new roof, huh? He didn't know whether or not he should laugh or be mad, so he decided to laugh. They all did.

"Does my mother know…uh…that?" Cody asked.

"No way. I told her that it was a grant for historical ranches."

Cody laughed until his sides hurt. He didn't know how long it had been since he'd laughed that hard, but it felt good.

When he finally stopped, Laura asked, "Ready to go, gentlemen?"

"Do we have to?" Johnny sang the words in a perfect whine.

"You heard your mother, partner," Cody said. "Always listen to your mother."

"I do." Johnny picked up his ball and tossed it in the air.

"All the time?" Cody asked.

"Most of the time."

Laura grinned as they approached. "I'd agree with 'most of the time.'"

Funny, Cody thought, *how I could picture the three of us as a family.* How could Johnny's father miss out on such wonderful times? What the hell was wrong with him?

Johnny reached for his hand, and Cody felt his jail-hardened heart turn to mush. The little guy's small hand in his made him feel… invincible.

He'd let the Liz Stevensons of the world think what they wanted to about him. He'd let the J. W. Dukes of this world work him like a rented mule. He'd break his back on the Double M, if only he could be with Laura and Johnny like this again and feel as though time hadn't passed him by.

They walked to the parking lot and split company. Laura was in the front of the paved lot; Cody was way in the back in the unpaved desert.

She offered him her hand, and in front of everyone, he briefly shook it. Then he shook hands with Johnny and headed for his truck.

He noticed that Liz Stevenson was watching them, and he couldn't help waving at her. She turned her back on him.

"That was a dumb thing to do," he admonished himself later as he climbed into the Double M's ancient truck. It was like waving a red flag in front of a bull, but he couldn't help himself.

He hoped that Mrs. Stevenson wouldn't run to J. W. Duke and tell him that he'd been with Laura and Johnny. There'd be hell to pay.

Laura didn't know when she'd be able to see Cody again. It had been difficult just getting him to go to the picnic and to bid on her basket.

But everyone who ever saw Cody and her together in the past, especially Liz Stevenson, could see through their plan.

So would her parents.

After she tucked Johnny into bed and answered nonstop questions about Cody being in jail, he finally went to sleep.

Tired herself, she poured herself a big glass of lemonade and headed for her room.

The phone rang and she answered. "Laura, I'd like to see you in my den, please. I'll send Clarissa over to watch Johnny while we talk."

Please? Her father never said "please," least of all to her.

A half-hour later, she knocked on the open door of his den. "Yes, Dad?"

"Sit."

"Am I a dog?"

"Please, sit."

Laura always liked his office/den. It smelled of old cigar smoke—even though her mother wouldn't let him smoke in the house anymore—and leather. Bound first editions decorated the shelves on three sides of the room. She'd read them all. J.W. hadn't read any, with the possible exception of *Moby Dick*.

She slid into a plaid armchair with a high back and took a sip of lemonade that she'd brought from her cottage.

"What's up, Dad?" she asked, holding her

breath. Liz Stevenson, or some other busybody at church, must have called him.

"How was the church picnic?"

"Fine. I had a good time. So did Johnny."

"And what about our gift?"

"The parishioners were overjoyed, and Reverend Pangburn had tears in his eyes." Laura smiled.

"Good. Good." J.W. chuckled. "I would have loved to see everyone's face. Dirt-poor cowboy makes it big and rubs their noses—"

"Dad! Is that what all your charity is about? And here I thought that you enjoyed giving—"

Her heart sank. How much more could her father disappoint her? She liked it better when they had been poor. They'd had a great time as a family. Even Penny didn't spew vile things the way she did now.

Oh, well. At least his money was doing some good.

"You could have gone in my place, Dad. You

could have stood before all the church people and gloated, if that's what you wanted."

"Of course that's not what I want. You aren't listening to me, Laura. You're just like your mother."

"Should I take that as a compliment?"

"Take it any way you want."

"Dad, I'm tired. And I don't want to play any more games today. Everyone accepted your gift with happiness and joy in their hearts. The church roof will be like new and the organ will play joyful music again thanks to you. I think that's what they are going to do with the matching funds."

He nodded. "Laura, there's something else I want to speak to you about."

"Yes. I know. Liz Stevenson got to you."

"Who?"

"You know, Liz Stevenson. Her husband, Gary, runs the sawmill out on River Road. She's not a very nice church lady."

"I don't believe I know her."

"Then it's not about Liz?"

"No. It's not about Liz." He leaned forward.

Oh, she almost blew it. If Liz Stevenson hadn't blabbed to him about her and Cody and Johnny, then who had?

"I'd like to talk to you about another donation, and I don't want you to say anything to anyone. Not your mother. No one."

She took a deep breath of relief.

"I promise, dad. What's up?"

"I want the foundation to somehow pay the Gonzalez kid's college tab. I think that his name is Reinnaldo or something."

"It's Alfredo. Do you want to fund all four years?"

"Yep. All four. Make up a scholarship or something, then see to it that he gets it."

"Okay, Dad. That's very nice of you."

He grunted. "Maybe I'll get more work out of Slim if he ain't worried about his kid. He tells me that Alfredo will be the first on both sides of his family to go to college."

"You know, dad, sometimes you have a soft spot that you don't want anyone to see. Why not?"

She'd wondered about that a million times.

"Then people take advantage of you. I don't like that. I'd rather just be anonymous."

The door squeaked open and the sudden noise made Laura jump.

"Momma?"

"Johnny? You're supposed to be home, taking a nap. What are you doing here?" Laura asked.

"I'm scared. I told Clarissa that I wanted my mommy."

"Why, honey? There are no monsters in your room." That was yesterday's problem.

"I'm scared of going to jail if I'm bad. I don't want to go to jail like Mr. Masters."

"Like who?" boomed her father.

Laura closed her eyes. *This can't be happen-*

ing. And she'd been worried about Liz Stevenson? She should have worried about Johnny.

"You aren't going to go to jail, sweetie," Laura said. "You haven't done anything wrong except for not staying in bed, and they don't put little boys in jail for that."

She took Johnny's hand and was just about ready to exit with him when J.W. said, "Oh, no, you don't. I want to talk to my grandson."

Grinning, Johnny ran to J.W., and J.W. lifted the boy onto his lap.

"What about Cody Masters, Johnny?" J.W. asked.

"It's nothing, dad. Don't cross-examine Johnny. If you want to know something, just ask me."

"Fair enough," J.W. said.

As Johnny doodled on a fresh piece of paper that J.W. set in front of him, Laura told her father how Cody had bid on her anonymous basket and won.

"And we ate lunch together, Grandpa, because it's the rule," Johnny said. "And we played catch. We had a fun time and ate chicken that Clarissa made and pie that Momma made."

J.W. grunted. "I see."

"Yes, it was the rule," Laura echoed. "And they had a great time playing catch."

"And Cody told Johnny all about being in jail?" J.W. smoothed Johnny's hair.

"He just answered Johnny's questions. Cody didn't say anything…inappropriate."

"Thank goodness for that. At least the man has some kind of sense."

"He has a lot of sense. If only you'd come to yours, Dad."

Her father lifted Johnny down. "Go home now, son."

"That's what Cody calls me, Grandpa. He calls me 'son.'"

J.W. eyes flared as he looked at Laura. "Put

Johnny to bed! And tend to that scholarship for the Gonzalez kid."

"Or?"

"Or stay here and explain yourself to me!"

"Then I'll see about the scholarship."

"We haven't finished talking about this," he said.

"Tomorrow's another day. At Tara," she said quietly with a Southern Scarlett O'Hara accent.

And there would be another civil war starting at the Duke Ranch.

Chapter Seven

Cody wiped the sweat from his face and neck with a wet, white towel that he'd brought from home. At five at night, it was one hundred and fifteen degrees on the outside thermometer that was shaped like a roadrunner.

The ancient thermometer inside the barn showed it was only ten degrees cooler there, even with the industrial fans blowing from every corner of the barn, running up their electric bill.

Looking up, he could see light. The barn's

roof needed help. He supposed he could nail down a tarp for a while until they sold some livestock. Then he could replace the roof or nail shingles over it. Terra-cotta that would match the house was just too damn expensive.

After all, he wasn't J. W. Duke.

Then the Double M needed new rails around the corral. The ones up now were so dried out; they were splintered and weak. He didn't want to lose any of the three horses they had.

His mother was going to harvest some of the prickly pear fruit from their cacti with the same name. Then she and Cindy were going to make jelly and sell it at the farmer's market in town.

They weren't going to get rich on prickly pear jelly, but every little bit helped.

As he mucked out the stall of his favorite gelding, Midnight Blue, he was finding muscles that had been dormant. Now they were sore and achy, but it felt good. So did the sun on his bare back when he was working outside.

He couldn't take his shirt off at the Duke Ranch. J.W. wouldn't hear of it. They all had to wear golden-yellow T-shirts with a crown on the pocket and the Duke logo under it.

The Double M didn't really have a logo or a symbol. Just the two *M*s. Not exactly exciting.

And it wasn't worth having a sign on the door of his sun-bleached, ancient pickup. That would be worth more than the truck.

He thought of his day with little Johnny and Laura. It was great fun until Liz Stevenson remembered that he was a jailbird. It was good that Liz didn't say the *m*-word—for murder or manslaughter—around Johnny.

Cody couldn't stand to hear that Johnny thought that his stint in jail was "cool." He'd hope that he'd gently dispelled that idea with their conversation at the picnic.

Speaking of the picnic, no doubt when J.W.

found out that the three of them had been to-gether—and he would—there'd be hell to pay.

Actually, Cody couldn't blame J.W. He was told up front to stay away from Laura, and now Johnny, but J.W. had been telling him that his whole life. Now the other man had more ammo because he didn't want them associating with a known murderer.

Even Cody didn't want them to be tainted due to him. It wasn't good for their reputations. However, Cody would burst if he couldn't see them.

He just would see them when other people weren't around.

His mother walked into the barn and handed him a frosty glass of lemonade. "It's so good to see you back on the ranch, Cody."

"It's great to be here, Mom."

She looked so tired and much older. He wished he could turn back the clock and change the events that led up to Hank Lindy being shot.

But Hank Lindy deserved killing for what he'd done—slapping, punching and manhandling his mother in the way he had. Then he was about to focus his violence on ten-year-old Cindy. If Cody hadn't stepped in, who knows what Lindy would have done to her?

The bastard.

"Cody, I'm so sorry—" his mother began.

"Mom, don't."

Tears pooled in her blue eyes. "I shouldn't have married Hank. I didn't love him. But we were struggling so, and he had money and he paid a lot of attention to me and Cindy, and well…"

"You didn't know that he was a…a…" Cody was going to say every inmate's favorite word, but this was his mother he was talking to.

"I should have known. I should have seen the signs that he was abusive. And he was screaming at Cindy too much for no reason. You know that she is such a gentle soul. She started to withdraw, and then Hank found out that I'd talked to a lawyer outside Duke Springs and was going to divorce him, and he went berserk. Well…you know the rest."

He knew all this, but obviously his mother wanted to talk.

She blinked and the tears ran like little rivulets down her cheeks. Cody gathered her into his arms. She was nothing but skin and bones.

"If I knew when I married him how brutal he was, of course, I never would have done it. But he had everyone fooled."

"I didn't know, either, until that night," Cody whispered. "I don't know how I missed the signs."

"Oh, Cody!" She sniffed. "I hid it well."

He rubbed her back. "Mom, I knew you'd want to discuss this, and we can talk about it more, but please don't blame yourself. The blame lies with Lindy. He was the one responsible for the chain of events—him and him alone."

"But you lost more than three years of your life, and now everyone thinks that you are… are…a…"

Murderer. Cody's mother just couldn't say the word.

Cody knew that she'd never get over her guilt that it was her fault he became incarcerated. "It was worth it, Mom. I'd do it all over again if I had to."

She was losing it, and he hated to see his mother so upset, so he hugged her for a while, letting her cry, then changed the subject. "So what's for Sunday dinner? I am starving."

Georgianna wiped her eyes with the edge of her flannel shirt. "I thought I'd grill us steaks. We're still celebrating your return."

"Let's keep celebrating, huh?" Cody said. "But I have to get these stalls cleaned before dinner and do a couple of other things, like feed and water the horses, so scoot your boots, Mom."

"I'm boot-scooting!" his mother said, managing a smile. "I'll ring the triangle when it's ready."

He reached for her and guided her into a little two-step around the barn, and Cody had never felt so free, so goofy. It helped him to see her smile. It felt almost normal. The way they were before Lindy. And there was steak for dinner! He could taste it now.

"Mom, could you make your special onion rings?"

"You got it," she said, hurrying to the back door of the ranch house.

His mom still looked good for her age and what she'd been through. He wished she didn't have to work so hard, but that was the life of a rancher.

Cody also wished he could help her more, but his income from his job at the Duke Ranch was a good start. If only he could make more money somehow.

The real money was back in the Arabian barn and the horses that J.W. boarded for his big-shot millionaire pals. Cody was the best horse trainer in the business. His father had taught him. Maybe he could get a job training the Arabians, and he could develop his own clients—or steal them from J.W.

But the big shots would take one look at the Masters' barn and head for the hills. They wouldn't want their expensive horses housed here.

"Another pipe dream," Cody said, spearing his pitchfork into a bale of hay. He gripped the wheelbarrow handles with his blistered hands and pushed it to the pile behind the barn, away from the house.

Yes, he was the best trainer in the business. If only he could teach horses how to use a toilet!

Just as he was feeding their horses, the triangle rang. It was probably Cindy ringing it because she loved to do so.

It was another little thing, but how he'd missed the sound of that iron ringing. Triangles like that had called cowboys in for meals as far back as anyone could remember.

He walked to the side of the barn and hosed himself off with the almost-too-hot water. As usual, there was a bar of soap on a chipped china saucer, and he washed his hands and face. There was no towel, so he dried off with his T-shirt, then slipped it on over his head. Due to the desert sun still overhead, he'd be dry before he hit the back door of the ranch house.

Cindy was flipping the steaks on the grill.

"Make mine rare, sis."

"I know. You haven't been gone that long that I'd forget."

He hugged her close. "Have you been okay?"

"Yeah."

"Still going to counseling?" he asked. His mother had written him and said that they'd found a counselor that they liked. They were going to both individual and group sessions.

"Yeah. I like her. Miss Dowd. She's nice."

"Do you still have nightmares, Cindy?"

"Yeah. The shots—they were so loud—and the blood and all. There was blood all over, Cody. Me and Mom scrubbed and scrubbed, but we couldn't get it out. Finally, we threw everything away. All of Lindy's stuff, too. And we bought a new rug for the living room floor."

"I know, sis, and I'm sorry. I'm sorry that you had to go through that. But it's done. He's gone. And he'll never bother you again."

Cindy shuddered. "There were other things before that. He'd squeeze my arm real tight, and he'd slapped me in the mouth a couple of times. Sometimes, he'd sneak up on me and put his hands around my throat. He told me never to tell Mom or he'd hurt her." She paused. "And then you had to go to jail. I've missed you so much, Cody."

He smiled. "I had to go. You know that. Now I'm on parole, you're going to counseling with Mom, and everything's going to be fine."

"I'm going to get a job, too, Cody. You'll see."

"Where do you want to work?"

"At the Duke Springs Bakery. My friend, Joanie's mom owns it, and she said that she'd give me a job when I turn sixteen in three years."

"Three years? You have a long wait, sis!"

"If I have papers, I can work earlier than that. I thought I could ride my bike to the bakery, so no one has to take me."

"You've got it all planned, huh?"

"Yeah. Sometimes I think that I want to get away from here, if only for a while."

"And sometimes you'll find that you can't wait to get back."

"Yup. I know." Cindy smiled.

Cody loved when she smiled. Before Lindy, she used to smile all the time. But back then, he'd still wished Cindy and his mother would have told him what Lindy was doing to them. He would have had a little "discussion" with the poor excuse for a man.

"Hey, sis, watch my steak. I want it still mooing!"

She laughed and put it on a plate. "Here you are. One mooing steak."

"Perfect," Cody said. "See you inside. I'm going to eat all the onion rings."

"Don't you dare!"

Finally, they all sat down and bowed their heads in thanksgiving. Then the good-natured teasing started between Cody and Cindy.

It was like he'd never been away.

"You know, Cody, I've been thinking," Cindy said.

"Don't hurt yourself," Cody joked.

"I've been thinking that Johnny Duke looks

an awful lot like you when you were his age. Have you looked at that picture of you on the wall in the hallway lately?"

"Cynthia Louise Masters!" Georgianna shook her head. "Keep your opinions to yourself, please."

"But, Mom, you know it's true. Cody and Johnny look like father and son. Laura said she met Johnny's father in college. I don't think that's the truth."

"What?"

Cody dropped his fork on the floor. He didn't bother to pick it up, but went straight to the hallway's picture gallery.

His heart pounded in his ears, and adrenaline slammed into his body just like it did when he was riding a bull.

He knew exactly the picture that Cindy was talking about. He was riding his first horse, Max, on his fourth birthday, and his father was standing alongside Max. Cody had a grin from ear to ear, just like the grin that Johnny sported when he talked about Pirate.

How could he have missed the fact that Johnny was the spitting image of himself at his age?

Nah. Cindy must be mistaken.

He went back to the table and sat down, dazed.

"Mom? What do you think?" Cody asked.

"I think that you need to have a serious conversation with Laura, Cody."

"I did. She said that Johnny's father was a college guy that she had a fling with."

Cindy munched on an onion ring. "You know… Laura has never had another boyfriend but you. She wouldn't…uh…be with another man. Not her. And when you were gone, she always visited and brought Johnny. I think she sneaked because J.W. and Penny don't like us, but she always let us babysit. In fact, I'm supposed to watch Johnny on Friday."

Cody tried to swallow the lump in his throat. "Mom? Tell me, please."

"You need to find the truth out from Laura. End of discussion. Are you going to eat your steak, Cody?"

"I lost my appetite. Save it for me for later, please. I have something to do right now."

"Please don't go charging over there," Georgianna pleaded. "It won't do any good. Can't you just wait until you see Laura?"

He checked the clock on the wall. "I'm going to see her right now. How could she keep something like this from me? And why am I so stupid that I didn't figure it out for myself?"

The screen door banged shut behind him, and as he was walking away, he heard his mother say, "Cindy, how could you?"

"Mom, if I'm wrong, I'll apologize and make it up to him ten times over. But if I'm right, Laura has a lot of explaining to do, and Cody's going to be hurt—and it'll be the worst kind of hurt."

* * *

Laura had to talk to Cody. She had to tell him to stay away from her and Johnny for a while. If J.W. heard one more word from Johnny about how wonderful Cody was, it wouldn't bode well for him.

Johnny was just enthralled with Cody. It made things worse when Johnny was visiting Pirate, and Slim Gonzalez told Johnny that Cody Masters was the best horseman he'd ever seen. Slim went on to say that Cody could teach riding, train horses and take care of them like a vet.

That's all Johnny needed. At dinner, he asked J.W. if Cody could teach him how to ride. Seemed as if her son wasn't satisfied just sitting on Pirate and being walked around the corral with Slim holding on to a lead rope.

Johnny wanted to be "a real cowboy like Cody."

Ouch! J.W. had steam coming out of his ears

after that little nugget was dropped over a meal of prime rib, baked potatoes and asparagus with hollandaise sauce.

After Johnny climbed up onto his grandfather's lap and asked him so sweetly, J.W. was putty in the little boy's hands. J.W. was ready to sign over the ranch to Johnny right then and there.

But instead, against his better judgment, he reluctantly agreed that Cody could give Johnny riding lessons on a trial basis. "Once a day for a half hour, and that's it."

Penny just sniffed, and huffed, and finally whispered to J.W., "Are you going to let your grandson be exposed to that…that…killer?"

"I've known Cody all his life, and he's not a killer," Laura whispered back.

Penny took a deep breath. "After Mike died, we should have offered Georgianna a lot more money for that run-down property, and maybe they all would have moved far away from Duke

Springs. She turned down our first offer. We should have upped the money. Anyone can be bought."

"Mother, please!" Laura raised her voice. "Not now!"

"You know I'm right."

"I don't know any such thing," Laura said, standing. "Please excuse me."

She went up to her old room to get her denim jacket. She ran a brush through her hair and touched up her makeup. She was thinking how glad she was that she'd never told Cody that Johnny was his son.

Cody would want to spend every minute he could with Johnny, and that would put Cody in the direct path of her parents.

She couldn't expose Johnny to their continued hatred of the Masters family, and constantly running interference would be even more exhausting than it already was.

Yes. She was right not to tell him.

* * *

The window shade of Laura's cottage was up halfway. That was their signal.

Thank goodness. She was going to meet him tonight. They had important matters to discuss, life-altering matters.

Cody sat on his usual rock, waiting for Laura to arrive. While he waited, he'd have a chance to cool down in the evening darkness and calm down before he busted a gut.

He thought of many different ways to approach Laura with the question of Johnny's paternity, but all of them sounded as if he was accusing her of sleeping around.

Hearing her approach, he stood, waiting for her to get closer.

At last, she emerged from the desert vegetation and was walking down the path to the creek.

"Laura, I'm glad you were able to come. I need to speak to you. It's very important."

"I don't think I can take anything else today. I'm just drained."

"I don't care how drained you are, dammit. I need to know if Johnny is my son." He didn't mean to blurt it all out like that. Out of a hundred scenarios, that one wasn't even in the running.

Laura stood on the path, probably deciding whether or not to run.

She took a deep breath. "Yes. Yes, he is. Johnny is your son, Cody. He's *our* son."

He couldn't breathe, couldn't swallow. He sat back down on the rock before he fell on his face into the shallow water.

"Why, Laura? Why didn't you tell me?"

"I couldn't take the chance, Cody. J.W. would see to it that you'd never get out of jail…ever. If he hadn't, my mother would have."

"They would deny me my son?" Cody asked. "Their hate goes that deep?"

"You couldn't support us, Cody. J.W. takes

great stock in that. I made up the college-guy story so they wouldn't take it out on you."

"My mother would have taken you in."

She wiped her tears on her sleeve. "Oh, believe me, I thought of Georgianna, but if you recall, they were going through a living hell of their own. Cindy was a mess and your mom was worse. I couldn't barge in like that."

"You still could have told me. Me of all people, Laura."

"And you'd be a basket case in jail not being able to be with Johnny. I couldn't bring him to see you. In fact, you banned me from visiting you."

"You could have told me sooner. When I got out."

"When, Cody? When was a good time?"

"And I'm so damn dumb, I sort of believed the college-guy story because I never thought you'd lie to me about such an important subject like my son. Then Cindy told me to look at a picture of myself at the same age," he said. "I can't believe I really didn't put it all together way before. I believed you, Laura. I believed you found someone else, just like I'd told you to."

She put her hand on his, and Cody almost shook it off. He wasn't ready for her to make a nice gesture. He was still in a world of hurt and anger.

She sighed. "Do you remember helping me move into the dorm in Phoenix? We made love on that tiny single bed. Your feet hung over the edge a mile. We laughed and laughed. Making love with you was fun, and loving and tender… all at the same time. Thinking of that day got me through nine months of lies and seeing you handcuffed and taken to jail the day of your sentencing."

"I want to move far away from Duke Springs," he snapped. "Me, you and Johnny.

Far away from your parents. We'll start over. We can learn to trust one another again."

She was being choked by tears. "Trust? Do you think we could ever trust each other again, Cody?"

He thought for a while. "I hope so, but we have to get out of here. We'll go north."

"You're a cowboy, Cody. Not a lobsterman or a dairy farmer. What would we live on? And you don't want to leave Cindy and your mother. They need you. Besides, you have to stay here for at least two more years because of your parole requirements."

"I could get a job in a factory in Phoenix or Tucson."

She grunted. "You'd hate that. It'd be like you're back in jail. I can't do that to you. Believe me, I thought of every possible way that we could be together. We'll just have to save every penny we can. Then maybe you can buy some livestock like you've always wanted, and you could supply rodeos with animals."

"It would take forever," he snapped, then thought for a while. "You know, Laura, I can understand why you hid Johnny from me in a way, but I don't know if I can ever forgive you."

"I did what I had to do, Cody." She gazed into his eyes. "Now, why don't you tell me what happened the night Hank Lindy died."

"Laura, don't ask me about that. I want to forget about it."

She raised an eyebrow. "I thought we were trying to trust one another."

He took a deep breath. "You're just going to have to settle for what you already know for now, okay? Trust me?"

"I'll try, Cody. I'll certainly try."

"Good." He clapped his hands. "Now, how can I see my son more?"

"How about if you give him riding lessons? A half-hour a day. It's already a done deal. Only, you can't tell Johnny you're his father. Not yet. Please, Cody. We'll figure out a good time."

"If it's a chance to be with my son, then I'm there. But I'm going to tell you one thing, Laura. I'm not going to wait much longer to be Johnny's father—his real father. We've both already lost too much time. And it's going to be out in the open. Let the chips fall where they may."

"I'm afraid of those falling chips, Cody. Really afraid."

Chapter Eight

Cody wanted to storm into J.W.'s office and tell him that he was Johnny's father. He was tired of tiptoeing around the man. He'd done that since his father had died.

Mike Masters wouldn't have been meek and mild like Cody. He'd call the man out and they'd fight. But Cody wasn't about to fight J.W., and he didn't want to argue with Laura. He'd let her have her way, just for a while. Then when Cody couldn't tolerate it anymore, he'd have to tell Laura that it was time that they both presented a united front against her parents. If she couldn't do that, then he would.

He thought he'd lost his man parts in jail, but this was so much worse.

Turning the light on in the barn, he headed for the right corner and the punching bag hanging from a crossbeam. He slipped on his boxing gloves and punched the hell out of the bag, trying to release some of his frustration.

He finally stopped when the sweat was pouring off him and his shoulders were burning. Then he hosed himself off and walked to the front porch to sit and think.

If only his father were here. Cody could talk to him better than anyone else in this world. He was dad, guidance counselor, priest, teacher and jail warden all rolled into one, and he'd oozed love from every pore.

He wanted to be a father to Johnny the way Mike had been to him.

Cody could talk to his mother about some

things. Maybe this was one of those. Maybe she could explain Laura's thinking to him.

He didn't know if his mother was definitely keeping Laura's secret, but it seemed as if she knew—or just guessed correctly.

Even his thirteen-year-old sister figured it out.

He didn't know he'd had to buy a clue.

In spite of all the complications, Cody grinned. He was little Johnny's father, and Johnny was a wonderful kid.

He was a dad, and he was going to be a real dad in every sense of the word!

The next afternoon, Laura watched as Cody helped Johnny brush Pirate. She could see the bunching and relaxing of the muscles in his back as he moved. Her cheeks flamed hot whenever she thought of Cody naked and making love to her.

It had been so long.

Right now the tension between them was like a thick fog that she couldn't see her way through. She wanted everything to go back to "normal" so badly, like when they were still in high school and sneaking around behind her parents' back.

In college, she had a taste of freedom before she had to drop out due to her pregnancy. She'd been twenty-three and tired. Tired of sneaking around. Tired of lying. Tired of getting lectured to by her parents since she became pregnant.

All she wanted was to start her own little family with Johnny and Cody.

Dreams do come true, she thought. *Don't they?*

After his stint at the Duke Ranch, mucking the barn at the Double M and taking care of the animals, Cody must have dozed off on the rocking chair on his porch, because the howling of wolves woke him up.

Going inside, he wiped the sleep from his eyes, thinking how he couldn't wait for tomorrow to come so he could be with Johnny again. It'd be a half-hour lesson, but Cody could stretch it to more with the added time of Johnny brushing down Pirate and cleaning the tack.

Of course, he'd help the little guy and maybe he could even play a little catch with Johnny. He seemed to like that.

J.W. must be softening a little if he was going to let Cody teach Johnny to ride. Obviously, Laura had arranged it.

And with any luck, J.W. wouldn't be around the next day so he could get to know his son, but that was too much to hope for.

Laura awoke the next morning, thinking that this was going to be the day that Johnny would be getting his first real riding lesson on Pirate.

She couldn't wait to see Cody again. They

still had a lot to discuss, but the biggest secret had been told. She felt as if the weight of
carrying it for almost four years had been
lifted.

Well, half lifted. She still had her parents to
tell—someday.

Today was going to be a great day! She'd
hang around the corral on the premise of
watching Johnny, but she'd be really watching Cody and their son together.

Just then, she heard beeping—the sound
made when trucks backed up. She looked out
of her bedroom window and saw an eighteen-
wheeler backing up to the patio.

Oh, no! She was going to be sick.

She'd forgotten today was the day of her
mother's card party and luncheon. It was a
benefit for the library in downtown Duke
Springs, the library that her great-grandmother
on her mother's side had helped build.

The Duke Foundation had paid for constant

updates to the building: new wiring, computers, networks, internet, and set up a little café in the corner that added a handful of jobs.

This benefit was for books, audio books, games and whatnot.

Laura was expected to be there and to give a speech as to what exactly the Duke Foundation had funded—undoubtedly for her mother to showcase her generosity—and what the organization planned to do next year.

She was also expected to greet the guests and charm them into giving more.

The same women—mostly shop owners—came to every fundraising event that the Dukes gave. It was the chance to be seen in the latest fashions and jewelry and to catch up with their neighbors and gossip. These ladies were mostly the same ones who were at the church picnic and saw her lunching with Cody.

Laura wasn't being bitter, but she was sure they were checking on the Dukes to report back to their husbands. The family's activities were great fodder for gossip during cocktail hour around their respective pools and at Pat's Honky-Tonk and Café on Interstate 36.

By the time she showered and dressed in her red-and-pink floral sundress with matching red lace espadrilles, fixed her hair in an upswept ponytail, put on some light makeup, picked out jewelry and made it downstairs, the truck was pulling out and the caterers were hard at work.

The event would be outdoors by the main house under a white canopy with fans to keep everyone from baking under the sun. It was an early event—eleven o'clock in the morning—due to the heat as the day progressed.

White tablecloths were being unfurled onto a couple dozen round tables. Chairs had matching white slipcovers with white bows in the back.

Heaven forbid that her mother's guests sat on metal folding chairs.

A brightly decorated van arrived from Rosie's Flowers. Beautiful centerpieces were unloaded and set on the tables for the usual raffle at the end of the event.

"Here you are, Laura," said Penny. "I was wondering when you'd get here. Clarissa has been keeping your breakfast warm for you."

"I must have been tired."

"You must have been out fairly late."

Laura's face flamed. "I sat outside for a while on the porch of my cottage. I couldn't sleep." That wasn't a lie; she did sit for a while on the porch of her cottage...thinking.

Penny eyed her from the tip of her hair to the bottom of her shoes. If she was going to say more, she didn't. She was distracted by some table that was missing a centerpiece.

Laura took a deep breath and went into the house to find Johnny. He was having breakfast with his grandfather. J.W. was reading the paper, and Johnny was reading from a Dr. Seuss book…er, he was making up a story from the pictures.

"And then the Cat in the Hat made a mess and the goldfish almost fell and…and… Hi, Mom!"

"Hi, sweetie. Did you sleep like a bug in a rug at Grandma and Grandpa's house?"

He giggled. "Like a bug in a rug."

J.W. folded his paper and set it down on the table. "Isn't he too old for that kind of talk?"

Here we go again—another disagreement about Johnny.

Instead of responding, Laura decided to ignore him.

"So, Johnny," she said, taking a seat next to him and pouring herself some coffee from a carafe. "You're going to have your first real riding lesson today."

He nodded like a bobble-head doll.

"It'll be cool, Mom. I like Mr. Masters. He's cool, too."

J.W. grunted. "That's not how I'd describe him."

"Dad, stop."

"Oh, all right. But I would have taught Johnny how to ride."

"So would I, but we're both too busy to give him lessons. Besides, I want him to learn correctly, and Cody is noted for his horse skills. You know that. Matter of fact, I don't know why you have him mucking out stalls. He should be in the A and B barns with the Arabians."

J.W. rubbed his chin as if he was thinking about it, but he quickly dismissed the thought with the wave of his hand. "I can't put him there. Our clientele wouldn't like it."

"Yes, they would. Especially when they see the results of Cody's excellent training on their expensive horses."

She might as well plant the seed. She knew her father would put his differences with Cody aside for the good of his ranch, not for her.

Maybe her father would think Cody was good enough for her when the millionaires did.

She hoped that Cody realized that she was always thinking, always planning. With her parents, she had to circle around them and catch them off guard, like a sneak attack.

Laura took a sip of coffee. "Sweetie, when you're ready, we'll go to the barn and see if Cody can give you your lesson now."

"I'm ready!" he said.

J.W. went back to reading his paper. "I'll stop by the corral and see how you're doing."

"Okay, Grandpa." Johnny scrambled down from his chair, and J.W. bent over to give him a kiss on the cheek.

"Tell Masters to keep an eye on my grandson. I don't want him hurt," J.W. bellowed.

Laura gave her father a kiss on the cheek and

whispered in his ear, "You can be assured that Cody wouldn't want Johnny hurt, either. He'll take good care of him."

"See to it," J.W. said, taking a sip of coffee.

Laura reached for a piece of toast and took her coffee with her. She had an hour before the first guests arrived, and she was going to enjoy it with Cody and Johnny.

Johnny insisted on putting his cowboy boots on and his cowboy hat. He said that "he wanted to look just like Mr. Masters."

Oh, you do, my little boy. You do.

Laura walked past all the tables with Johnny. She had to admit, everything looked beautiful. Where she would be sitting, at the head table, she'd have a perfect view of the barn. Maybe she could catch glimpses of Cody and Johnny during the riding lesson.

As Laura and Johnny approached the barn, Cody appeared, leading Pirate into the corral.

Johnny waved excitedly. "Hi, Mr. Masters. Hi, Pirate."

"Hello, son," Cody replied, and Laura's heart did a flip in her chest at that simple greeting, which had much more meaning now.

Cody turned to her. "Everything okay?"

"Yes. How about you?"

"Been doing a lot of thinking."

"Anything you want to share?"

He shook his head slightly, then gave Johnny his full attention. "Are you ready to ride your horse, Johnny?"

"Well, yuh!"

"Well, yuh!" Cody echoed, giving Johnny a high five.

Johnny climbed over the fence, and Laura was about to reprimand him, but Cody said, "The first thing that you need to know is that you don't come near Pirate or the barn unless I say so."

"Okay, Mr. Masters."

"So, Johnny, you can climb the fence this time, but the next time, go through the barn and make sure I'm with you. Okay?"

As she helped Johnny up, Laura was pleased at Cody's care.

Cody lifted Johnny and set him down in the corral. Then he squatted down to talk to the boy. "Pirate's a nice pony. He'll take you anywhere after I teach you, and I'm going to do a little training with Pirate, too."

"Cool."

"Definitely cool," Cody answered. "Uh… Johnny…do you mind if I give you a hug?"

Johnny hesitated, and Laura held her breath. This could go either way. If Johnny rejected him, Cody would be hurt.

But he didn't. Cody reached up and wrapped his arms around the boy, picking him up. He closed his eyes, as if he was absorbing every inch of his son.

Tears fell down Laura's cheeks, and she had nothing to wipe them off but her fingers.

Cody set Johnny down and handed Laura a red bandanna that he pulled from the pocket of his jeans.

He whispered to her, "I love him, and I don't even really know him."

"You will. I promise," she replied.

"You look incredibly beautiful today," he said softly, and his words sent little shivers down the back of her neck. "Tonight?"

"Of course." She couldn't wait until dusk.

He nodded, then turned to Johnny. "I'm going to show you how to saddle Pirate the right way. We'll do it together."

Laura heard her mother call her name. "I have to go, Cody. Have a good time, Johnny, and listen to what Mr. Masters tells you."

"I will!"

Laura looked for her mother and found her with a group of women.

"Here's my lovely daughter now. Laura, my generous friends would like to write checks to the library fund. When are we going to collect them?"

Laura turned to the well-heeled attendees. "I'll collect your checks at the end of the luncheon, ladies, and if you forget, I'll certainly remind you."

There was giggling amongst the group. Laura had to admit that she was good at schmoozing with the guests, but she just wasn't in the mood for a garden party, no matter how nice it was going to be.

She'd rather be in her jeans and at the barn with Cody and Johnny.

As she turned to walk to her seat at the head table, she saw J.W. heading to the corral.

Here he comes.
Cody was leading Pirate around the corral with Johnny on the saddle.

"Keep your feet straight, cowboy. Don't let them bounce around. Pirate won't know what command you are giving him. Do you know what I mean by command?"

Johnny shook his head. "Nope."

"He won't know what you want him to do. You tell Pirate what to do with the reins and with your heels, and sometimes clicks or some other kind of noise from your mouth. Know what I mean now?"

"I get it, Mr. Masters."

Cody could see J.W. leaning on the fence; he tried to ignore him and concentrate on Johnny, but there was so much on his mind, it was overwhelming.

"Good job in keeping your feet from bouncing around, Johnny."

He was going to meet Laura again tonight.

Johnny was his son.

When could he tell the world that Johnny was his son?

When could he and Laura get married?

Would they live at the Double M?

Could he last for two years at the Duke Ranch?

Would his parole officer let him work somewhere else?

On and on his thoughts went, but one thing that he knew was that he loved Laura and had always loved Laura. Now he loved Johnny.

But the altercation with Liz Stevenson reminded him that most of the community considered him a killer—a murderer. How could he blame them?

And how could he subject Laura and Johnny to their taunts and jeers?

He shouldn't.

If he was any kind of man, he'd walk away. He'd just disappear. He didn't know who'd hire an ex-con for any decent kind of job, but he could send money to his mother for the Double M and to Laura for Johnny's support. Maybe he could pick crops. It was backbreaking work for little money, but he was used to that.

Hopeless. He couldn't see any way out.

"Nice riding, Johnny," J.W. yelled.

"I'm trying to keep from kicking Pirate, Grandpa. Mr. Masters says that it's important."

"He is correct."

"I'm going to be a cowboy like Mr. Masters."

"What about being a cowboy like me, Johnny?" J.W. puffed on his cigar.

"Sure, Grandpa. You, too."

"Your grandfather is a good cowboy, Johnny," Cody said. "Look at the ranch he built."

If J.W. was taken aback, Cody was worse. Without thinking, he'd actually paid J. W. Duke a compliment.

"Uh…thank you, uh…Cody," J.W. said, grunting out the words through his cigar stub.

"I'm going to be a good cowboy, too," Johnny said.

J.W. chuckled and Cody passed in front of him with Pirate and Johnny in tow.

"Cody, is my momma a good cowboy?" Johnny asked.

"She's a good cowgirl. She can ride like the wind, and she always wanted to learn everything she could." He gave J.W. a pointed look and said, "Particularly about running this ranch."

J.W. seemed to get Cody's message, but chose not to comment. "Um, from what I can tell, you're doing a great job with my grandson. Keep it up."

"Should I take that as a compliment, Mr. Duke?"

"Take it any way you want." He puffed on his cigar. "When you're done, have Slim walk Johnny up to the house. Laura's busy with the garden party."

"I can walk Johnny up to the house," he said, knowing perfectly well what J.W. would say.

"Slim can do it. Get him. I'm sure you have a lot of work to do."

"Fine." He got the message. J.W. didn't want Cody near the ranch house. But he was sure that J.W. caught the sarcasm in his response. Their complimentary session was over.

J.W.'s eyes narrowed. "Do what I tell you, Masters."

Cody nodded. No Masters had been near J.W.'s ranch house in decades.

When he saw that Johnny was getting tired, Cody showed him the right way to get off Pirate, and Cody let Johnny lead the pony into the barn to brush and water him.

After that was completed and Pirate was tucked nicely into his stall, Cody gave a shout-out for Slim but couldn't find him anywhere.

"I'll take you to your mother," Cody decided.

Cody felt Johnny slip his hand into his, and he almost melted.

And off they walked to the ranch house under the glares, stares and astonishment of the ladies in attendance at the party, particularly Penny, and to the delight of Laura.

Chapter Nine

Penny paced back and forth along the border of pampas grass. "Did you hear everyone talking about Cody Masters? I was never so embarrassed in my life. For heaven's sake, half of them wanted to call the sheriff's department and have him put back behind bars, the other half wanted to sleep with him."

Count me among those who want to sleep with him, Laura thought, sipping iced tea as her mother paused.

"I don't want Cody with Johnny anymore, hear me?"

"Cody is teaching Johnny how to ride. If Dad and I don't have an objection, why is there suddenly a problem?"

"There isn't *suddenly* a problem. There's *always* been a problem with that man."

"I don't want to talk about it anymore, Mother. I want to take a walk with my son and listen to how excited he is to learn how to ride Pirate the right way and listen to every bit of what Cody told him. I'll take a sandwich along, since Johnny didn't have lunch yet, and we'll have a picnic and maybe he'll take a nap on a blanket. That's all I want to do right now."

Laura turned to go to the kitchen. "Oh, and maybe I'll say a little prayer for the hypocrites who pretend to be so charitable so they'll discover that charity isn't just about money."

* * *

"I am so sorry, Cody." Georgianna Masters Lindy stopped rocking, and turned to her son. "It seems like I can't stop apologizing to you… for everything."

"Mom, stop. It's not your fault. It was Laura's decision, and while I understand a lot of her reasoning, it still hurts. I missed almost four years of Johnny's life, four years! And I missed her pregnancy, too. And I would love to have been there for his birth."

Georgianna opened her mouth to tell him that she was sorry yet again, but Cody held his hand up. "Stop. Let's change the subject. I have to forgive Laura in my own time and in my own way."

"Talk to her, Cody. She'll tell you why she didn't tell you."

"Oh, we talked, and I suppose there will be more talking, and in time…" He shrugged. "I'm going for a walk."

"Is Laura at the creek?"

Cody whirled around. "You know?"

"Of course. That's where your father and I always met. His mother didn't particularly like me. It took her a while, but I won her over."

"You never told me that."

"Your grandparents lived with us, and it wasn't easy. Your grandmother, Tysia, was tough, and she loved to meddle in our affairs, but the worst part was that her apron strings were tied around your father's waist like a lasso around a steer. When we wanted a break and some alone time, we headed to the creek. It's the best thing on this ranch."

"See you later, Mom. Thanks for the conversation."

She got up from her rocker and kissed him on the forehead. "Go talk to Laura, and remember that you two are always welcome at the Double M."

"I know we are. Thanks."

"Johnny is comfortable here, too. Laura brought him over for visits whenever her parents weren't around. I think she wanted him to get to know us."

"So you knew, Mom?"

"Laura never told me, but I guessed. Johnny looked like you right from the start."

He was happy that Laura shared Johnny with his mother and sister, and he remembered that Cindy was supposed to babysit him on Friday, in a couple of days.

He wondered what Laura had to do that night. Better yet, that meant that her parents wouldn't be around. Maybe the two of them could have a real date and get to know each other again, maybe discuss their plans for the future and Johnny.

When he got to the creek, Laura and Johnny were on a blanket. Johnny was curled up against Laura's side, sound asleep. Laura was awake.

She motioned to him with an index finger against her lips that he should be quiet. Slowly, she pried herself away from their son, made him comfortable and then got up from the blanket.

Cody held out his arms, and she walked into them with a big sigh. He held her for what seemed like the longest time, waiting for her to speak.

"Thanks, Cody. I needed that."

"Happy to oblige. Anytime."

"Hey, I want to ask you out on a date Friday night. I have to speak at another fundraiser. This time, it's for the Duke Springs Nursing Home and Rehabilitation Facility, and it's at the hotel and conference center downtown. I asked Cindy to babysit because my parents will be at an auction in Phoenix, and it's Clarissa's day off. Will you go with me?"

He raised an eyebrow and grinned. "Is there food involved?"

"Lunch."

"Then count me in."

She laughed, then sobered. "Are you doing okay?"

He shrugged. "I'm still hurting, but I'll get over it."

"I did what I thought was best—I told you that—and that's what I'm still doing," Laura said softly.

"When do we tell your parents?"

"I want to wait for a while," she said.

"For what? Your parents are never, ever going to accept me. You might have to decide between Johnny and me, or them."

"I can't make that choice."

"Why not?"

Laura pushed her bangs out of her eyes. "I work for them at the Duke Foundation, for one. We do a lot of charity events. I don't want to give that up."

"If you lived at the Double M, I take it that you couldn't still work at the foundation."

"I thought about living there, but there's not enough room, Cody. And as for the foundation, you can be sure I won't be running that if I move to the Double M. My parents would take my job away faster than a roadrunner can run, but I can find another job."

"The three of us can live in my bedroom. It's small, but we could probably fit a twin bed in there for Johnny."

"A twin bed? How would we walk in there? And before you suggest it, the three of us can't sleep in the same bed," Laura said. "And five people using one bathroom?"

"It's not the White House, like your place, but it'll do."

"We'll have to come up with another plan. Like we'll have to save money and then maybe put up a double-wide trailer somewhere."

"It'll have to be on the Double M," Cody said.

"Yes. I know. And that means we're going to need a foundation and septic, electric and water. And then there's the cost of the dou-ble-wide."

"That's a lot of money, and I'm only getting a quarter over minimum wage," Cody said. "I've been putting my paycheck into the Double M, but I can change that."

"Cody, the good news is that I'm getting a cut of the interest from the Duke Foundation money for a salary. I can ask my folks for a raise. My investments have been steadily pay-ing off, so the fund is actually worth a lot more money than when I started. And it will get a boost from the annual Duke Ranch Rodeo. When the dust settles at the fairgrounds, all the money will go into the fund to replenish it, for a new day-care center and grammar school."

The Duke Ranch Rodeo! He'd forgotten about that!

He snapped his fingers. "I know how I can get us some money. I'm going to ride bulls at the Duke Ranch Rodeo!"

Laura shook her head. "You haven't ridden bulls for three or four years, Cody. What makes you think you can compete?"

"It's like riding a bike—"

"A bike won't stomp you and stab you with his horns. A bike doesn't weigh a ton, either."

"I'll get on some practice bulls here. Slim will let me, and—"

"You'll kill yourself. Besides, my father won't allow anyone to ride our bulls for practice. He says that it's unfair to the other contestants since he supplies the stock."

"Then I'll ride practice bulls somewhere else." He took her hand and grinned. "Maybe I'll win us some money."

"And maybe you'll end up in the hospital."

"Thanks for your faith in me."

"It's not a matter of faith, Cody. It's that I know you haven't been on the back of a bull for a long time."

"I was a world champ," Cody said, remembering good times riding the bull circuit with pals and finally scoring enough points to make it to Vegas. He'd had to retire early because his mother had needed him, but he'd felt free and happy for a while, chasing his dream.

He'd been trying to save his winnings to marry Laura, but then Hank Lindy came into their lives, and everything fell apart.

"That's my plan. It might be a long shot, but it's better than doing nothing." He chuckled. "And I don't want to get hurt, either. I don't have insurance."

Laura took a long, deep breath. "Oh no, Cody."

"Insurance costs too much money."

Laura shook her head. "Money, money—everything has to do with money, and I don't like it."

"But you have it, honey. You're used to the stuff. Some of us never had that problem but wish we did."

"I don't want to talk about money, Cody."

"Look." He reached for her hand and squeezed it. "I'll call my friend Skeeter Mc-Avoy. Skeeter has a good pen of bulls. I'm going to have to practice—and soon."

"And where are you going to find the time?"

"That's the problem. Maybe Slim will let me sneak out early the next couple of days and I can drive out to Skeeter's ranch."

"I really hope you win, Cody, and that you end up in one piece."

"I will, if you're there cheering for me."

"Of course, and Johnny will be with me."

She tipped her head up and their eyes met. Cody pushed aside the fact that Laura hadn't told him about Johnny, and that she wouldn't let him fully claim his son right now.

He pulled her toward him and wrapped his arms around her, holding her tight. This was his Laura, the girl he grew up with and whose pigtails he pulled. The Laura who grew into a woman, who gave him a son, whom he always knew he was meant to be with—forever.

He loved her. He'd always loved her. Their lips met, tentative at first, then he increased the pressure, and it was as if they'd never been apart.

They kissed and touched and when Johnny whined and woke up, they pulled apart.

They'd make it. Somehow.

All he had to do was win the bull-riding competition at the Duke Ranch Rodeo in a couple of weeks. First place would be worth at least fifty thousand bucks.

That kind of money would kick-start his future with Laura and Johnny.

Laura enjoyed her speaking engagements and always geared her speeches to the specific event.

The Duke Springs Nursing Home and Rehabilitation Facility was one of her favorite places that the Duke Foundation supported, and she did volunteer work there whenever she could. It was clean, comfortable and homelike.

The residents, along with their relatives and friends, were also invited to the luncheon at the conference center downtown, and the coordinator said that about three hundred people were expected.

That would be a nice crowd.

The rehab part of the facility wanted some modern equipment. The nursing home part wanted new rugs, some smart TVs and a couple of washing machines and dryers.

The Duke Foundation could cover all that. Plus, Laura had a surprise for them—an addition with a new indoor pool complete with lifts and ramps. She was going to work with the administrator and architects to give them exactly what they needed.

As she was dropping off Johnny for Cindy to babysit, Cody had just returned from riding practice bulls. He walked to meet her and moved as if he was sore, shuffling as though he should be at the rehab facility himself.

He lifted Johnny out of the truck, and it looked as if every bone and muscle in his body screamed for mercy.

Cody gave Johnny a kiss on the cheek, and Johnny didn't seem to mind.

"Hi, cowboy!" Cody said. "Haven't seen you since this morning. You did a great job on Pirate today. Pretty soon, I won't be holding the reins and leading Pirate."

"Really, Mr. Masters?"

"Really."

"That'll be cool."

Cody set Johnny on the ground, and Johnny ran to the porch. "Cindy?"

"She's inside, Johnny," said Georgianna. "She's setting up some kind of project for you two to do."

"Cool." Johnny swung open the front door and it banged against the house. He ran inside.

"Johnny really likes Cindy," Laura said to Cody.

"I can tell."

Just as soon as Johnny left, he ran back out to give Georgianna a hug.

"Hi," he said.

"Welcome, Johnny. I was wondering if I'd get a hug from you today." Georgianna gave him a kiss.

He ran back inside the ranch house. *Bang!* The screen door whacked against the house again.

"Go easy on the door, Johnny!" Laura yelled.

"Okay!" was Johnny's response from inside.

Cody chuckled. "I love to see that Johnny is so happy and comfortable at the Double M."

"I made sure that your mom and Cindy both knew him and saw him grow, and that he knew them."

"Thank you for that." Cody fell into step beside her as she walked to the Double M's ranch house. "Do your parents know that my mother and sister are babysitting Johnny tonight?"

"No way. They think Clarissa's sister is watching him because Clarissa has the day off. I didn't correct them."

Cody shook his head. "So you've been lying to them when you bring him over here?"

"Yes. It's become a habit."

"Someday you won't have to."

"That would be a miracle," she said.

Cody put his hand on the small of her back, and she immediately felt the warmth. She leaned into him.

"Want to check out my room for space?" Cody said.

Laura couldn't picture herself living at the Double M, but maybe she'd get used to it. She'd have to find another job other than running the foundation—*darn it*—and find trustworthy babysitters for Johnny. Cindy had school, and Georgianna was certainly busy.

Could she do that?

"Sure, let's go look at your room," she said. She remembered it from sneaking around with Cody in their younger days, but it'd been a while.

The room was way too small.

"Cody, do you think that Cindy would switch rooms? Hers is bigger."

He shrugged. "I could ask her. If it means Johnny living here, she'd jump at the chance."

"But remember, I won't have a job if I move out to live at the Double M. My parents would pretty much banish me."

"Even Johnny?" Cody asked.

"They'd file for visitation, if not custody. Remember?"

"No way would they get custody of my son!"

"But just think for a moment, Cody. They are pillars of the community, and you have a manslaughter conviction on your record. I'm an unfit mother who hangs around with a convict and subjects her son to you. Who do you think the court would give custody of Johnny to?"

"Dammit, Laura. Dammit!"

"Don't think about it now. Let's go to the event and enjoy ourselves. It's time for the community to see you again at another fundraiser. Someone will let the news slip to my folks, but I'll face them in the morning and explain that you were just attending because you know someone living at the nursing home." She grinned. "What a coincidence!"

She ran her fingers through his hair and tried not to look at Cody's bed.

In less than a second, they could be stretched out on it and making love.

Cody wanted to make love with Laura, but it was hardly appropriate in his mother's house. If they were married, it'd be another story.

That was some of what he considered his "cowboy code." Laura had always been his rock, his shelter from a storm, but he wasn't used to just sitting back and letting someone else take the reins, even if that person was her.

"Let's go to Cindy's room and take a look at it," he suggested.

"I'd hate to disrupt Cindy's life."

"We haven't. Not yet anyway. Let's just take a look."

In her bedroom, Cindy was reading to Johnny. He was sitting on a child-size recliner, and he seemed mesmerized at her every word.

"Cindy, I just wanted to thank you for taking care of Johnny tonight," Laura said.

"No problem. We are enjoying ourselves already. And later we are going to… *Oops!* I almost gave away our secret. Huh, Johnny? And here I thought that you'd be the one to give it away."

"I keep the secret of finger painting." Johnny grinned.

Cindy rolled her eyes, and they all laughed.

Laura noted that Cindy's room did have more space than Cody's. A twin bed could fit without everything being cramped. It would definitely do if it came to that, but Laura was still aiming for a double-wide trailer so they could be by themselves.

She might have to climb down from her high horse and get realistic if she wanted to become a family with Cody and Johnny.

If only her parents would let them live in her cottage, but she doubted Cody could survive on the Duke premises.

"Cody, hurry up and take a shower. You smell like livestock. Then we need to get going to the conference center," she said, then quickly explained to Johnny and Cindy. "It's where the event is. I'm going to speak in front of a lot of people, and I have to admit that I'm a little nervous."

"No need to be nervous," Cody said. "You're an excellent speaker, Laura. Very natural."

"Thanks." She gave Johnny a big kiss good-bye, and Cody did the same. Then he shook Johnny's hand and ruffled Cindy's hair—which resulted in a howl from her. Then he headed back to his room to take a shower and get ready.

Laura went out on the front porch to talk to Georgianna while she waited for Cody. Laura avoided all talk about Johnny being Cody's son.

Soon, they were in Laura's car headed for the Duke Springs Hotel and Conference Center.

They'd decided not to walk in together. That way, Laura could keep to her story that Cody was just an attendee.

He went in first, and wondered if he'd ever get used to the fact that people he'd known his whole life treated him as if he had the plague, while others felt that he'd paid his debt to society and was now a free man. Some shook his hand warmly, if somewhat warily. Others turned their back on him.

Sitting in the rear of the huge room at a table alone, he reminded himself that it was the Dukes who'd built this town and positioned it around two hot springs. Out of the seven or more hot springs that were in the area, J. W. Duke controlled six of them.

The last one was on Masters land, deep in the cottonwoods. Most of the time, it was barely a trickle, feeding into the creek. When he had the money, Cody would tap it and bring it out to its full capacity.

That was another reason why J.W. coveted the Double M land.

Cody looked around the meeting room at the conference center. Even that was top-notch. The hotel attached was a five-star property, and people came from all over to enjoy the hot springs. J.W. had hit the jackpot here.

What he wouldn't give to strip down and sit in one of those springs about now.

He could tell that Laura was looking for him. Every now and then, her eyes found him at his solitary table, and she'd smile. He'd smile in return.

She gave a brilliant speech, and the result was chuckling and downright belly laughs from the audience.

After announcing the very generous items that the Duke Foundation was donating, she received a standing ovation.

Then she reminded everyone about the Duke Ranch Rodeo at the fairgrounds that weekend. Funds would help build a day-care center and a new grammar school.

When she announced that work was going to begin on the in-ground rehab pool at the rehab facility, everyone who could stand got to their feet and cheered.

There were more speeches from other local dignitaries, most of which made him doze. None was as rousing as his Laura's.

As luck would have it, Cody was offered several desserts from waitresses on their way to the kitchen for refills, but every time the door swung open, Cody smelled something hot and greasy.

What are they cooking back there?

No sooner did he think that, when one of the waitresses came out coughing. Then she pulled the fire alarm on the wall.

"Fire!" she yelled. "Fire! Everyone get out!"

Chapter Ten

Since Cody was sitting by the kitchen, he could see flames licking at the door leading to the conference room. Suddenly, there was a stampede of attendees.

"Slow down!" he yelled, waving people to the exits. They were stumbling and tripping over the slower-moving wheelchairs and people on crutches.

Where was Laura?

The only exits that he could see were at the

double doors by him, and he hadn't seen her walk by.

"Laura!" he yelled. "Has anyone seen Laura Duke?"

No one answered. They were too busy shoving the person in front of them. Some kind souls did stop to help push wheelchairs and clear a path for those on crutches, but on the whole, the crowd was in a panic; they were just trickling out, and the smoke was getting thicker.

What was the holdup getting out of the room?

By now the fire had spread to the back wall by the exit doors.

Some people had stopped to talk in the hallway. How could they do that when there were more people that needed to get out of the room?

"Move it! Don't block the exit! Move!" he yelled and got a little cooperation.

"Don't touch those doors!" he shouted. "They're hot."

Cody moved as much of the crowd out of the room as he could until firefighters finally arrived. They tried to get in though the massive amount of people exiting. Cody detoured the crowd over a couple of feet so they could get to the fire.

"Kitchen." He pointed to the swinging doors leading to the kitchen. It was engulfed in flames. "Help me get these people out of here, will you?" he said to one firefighter nearby.

The smoke was thicker than fog. "Let's move it! No pushing, please!" Cody yelled. "Move!"

And all the time, he kept looking for Laura.

"Have you seen Laura Duke? Anyone seen Laura Duke?"

"She was in the ladies' room, the last I knew," yelled a voice from the crowd.

"Where?" asked Cody.

"To the right of the stage."

"Thanks."

Cody fought the crowd going in the opposite

direction to find Laura. The room was down a long hallway, and unfortunately, it shared a left wall with the kitchen.

Hurriedly, he pushed open the door to the ladies' room and yelled her name.

"Laura?"

He looked under the stalls and saw Laura lying on the floor, coughing.

Going to her side, he helped her turn over. "Honey, let's get you out of here."

Picking her up, he carried her to the exit doors. He was happy to see that, finally, the hotel staff had arrived on the scene and gotten the hallway cleared out. He was able to walk outside easily with a barely conscious Laura in his arms.

Cody gently laid her on the floor and pulled his jacket off to put under her head. An EMT set her up with oxygen.

"Let's get her to the hospital," the EMT said,

then spoke into a microphone clipped to the shoulder of his shirt.

Laura's eyes fluttered, then more coughing.

"It's good that she's coughing," the EMT said. "It clears her lungs. We'll get her to the hospital, and they'll give her some humidified oxygen."

Cody reached for her hand and squeezed it tightly. "You'll be okay, sweetheart. Don't worry."

She tried to talk but coughed instead.

"I'll go with you in the ambulance," Cody said. "Don't worry."

In a hospital wing that contained a plaque identifying her grandparents as contributors, Laura squeezed Cody's hand. "Cody, call Clarissa. Her number is on my cell. Ask her to pick Johnny up at the Double M tonight, and take him home to my parents."

Why isn't the Double M considered Johnny's home, too?

"Is your phone in your purse?"

Her eyes opened wide. "I don't have my purse!"

"It's at the hotel, isn't it?" He was so worried about Laura, he could have cared less about finding her purse.

She pulled her oxygen mask up. "It's where I was sitting," she said. "Hanging over my chair. Cody, my whole life is in that purse, and the big check to the nursing home is in it, and some—"

"I'll take care of it. I'll take care of Johnny. You just relax and breathe."

"Your mom knows Clarissa's number," she said.

"Rest, Laura. That's an order."

She opened up one eye.

"Okay, okay. Make it a request!"

Cody phoned the Duke Springs Hotel and Conference Center. After being transferred from one person to another several times, he finally got someone to find Laura's purse and bring it to her hospital room.

Then he sat and watched her sleep.

He knew that he should phone her house and tell her parents that she was in the hospital, but he was avoiding it. If they asked, he'd stick to the story that they came separately, and he'd stayed to listen to her speak.

He walked out into the hallway and looked out the window. It was monsoon season in Arizona, and it was raining like crazy. There would be no unnecessary travel in weather like this due to flash flooding. Taking a deep breath, he punched in the numbers of the Duke ranch house.

"Hello?"

It was Penny.

"Mrs. Duke, this is Cody Masters. Before you hang up, I need to tell you that Laura is in the hospital. Smoke inhalation. There was a kitchen fire at the hotel where she was speaking and she passed out from all the smoke."

"Oh no!" Penny started to cry.

"No, really. She's going to be okay. I'm with her at the hospital, and they are giving her oxygen. They are keeping her overnight to make sure everything is okay. If it is, she can be released in the morning."

"We'll be right up," she said. "J.W. and I."

"I'd advise you to stay where you are. It's pouring like crazy and you don't want to get stuck. Besides, Laura is sleeping right now and can't really speak due to the oxygen mask they have over her mouth. It's up to you, but you shouldn't drive in this."

"Since when do we listen to you?"

He swore under his breath before he could stop himself. "Never," he whispered. "You would never listen to me. But hey, it's up to you. Float here in a boat from Phoenix if you'd like and watch her sleep."

"Are you going to stay with her?"

"Yes, I am."

"J.W. isn't going to like that."

"Mrs. Duke, Laura almost died tonight on the floor of the ladies' room. Ask me if I give one damn what J.W. likes or doesn't like. I'm staying with Laura. Do what you want."

"Oh no! She almost died?"

"Yes."

"Did you find her?" she asked, her voice thin.

"Yes, I did."

"Then we owe you our thanks."

"You don't owe me anything, Mrs. Duke," Cody said. "If you'd like, I'll have Laura call you in the morning."

"Please do."

"Okay, good night."

"Cody?"

"Yes?"

"Thank you for saving our Laura, and thanks for calling."

"Of course. Good night."

Cody went back into the room. Laura was still sleeping but looked as if she was struggling to get the oxygen mask off her face.

He gently grasped her arm. "Leave it alone, honey."

"It's bothering me."

"It's clearing your lungs from the smoke."

"Okay."

"I told your mother that you were in the hospital. And now I'll call my mother and Cindy. Then I'll call Clarissa and tell her what happened."

"Thanks, Cody. You talking to my parents… that must have been difficult for you."

"Not exactly. Your mother put aside our differences for a while so I could tell her about you. Your father wasn't around. I imagine she'll tell him."

"Did she say anything about Johnny?" she asked.

"No. She thinks he's at Clarissa's house over-night. Remember?"

She nodded. "So many lies."

"Say the word and we can end it all."

She closed her eyes and Cody wondered if she was actually sleeping or just wanted to shut him up.

About an hour later, Cody heard excited chatter out in the hallway.

He walked out of the room and caught the attention of a nurse. "What's going on?"

"A couple is being helicoptered in from Duke Springs. It's the first use of the chopper pad on the roof. And the person who paid for the helicopter pad is the first to fly in."

"Would that be J. W. Duke?" Cody asked.

"You know him?" The nurse's face lit up.

"Doesn't everyone?" Cody couldn't muster any enthusiasm for the Dukes' arrival, and walked back into Laura's room.

He wondered briefly what he should do. He

could make up some lie and split. However, looking at Laura in the hospital bed, it didn't seem important to lie.

"Where's my daughter?" J.W.'s voice boomed.

"Room 137, Mr. Duke," Cody heard the same nurse say. "I'll show you."

"Thank you."

"It's right here, J.W.," said Penny.

Cody didn't want to deal with them. After everything that had transpired, he just didn't have the energy. He knew now how Laura felt. J.W. stood in the doorway, looking larger than life. "How's my daughter?" He had the sense to whisper after catching a glimpse of Laura sleeping.

Approaching the bed, he took her hand and shook his head. "I don't want to wake her."

Penny took Laura's other hand. "She almost died, J.W."

J.W. looked at Cody for verification. Cody nodded.

"I understand that we have you to thank for saving her life," J.W. said softly.

"I was glad I was there."

"And just *why* were you there?" J.W. said through gritted teeth.

"Let's not get into that right now. Not when Laura is like this," Cody said.

"You're right." J.W. held out his meaty right hand. "I suppose I should thank you, Cody."

Cody took a step back and debated if he should shake the man's hand. "I suppose you should." That was tacky of him to say, but he couldn't resist the comeback.

Cody finally offered his hand, and J.W. shook it. He thought that J.W. looked as if he'd aged ten years since he'd seen him last. Even though he had a hard time showing it, maybe he did care about Laura, after all.

"I'd like to thank you, too, Cody." Penny offered her hand and Cody took it. It was cold and clammy, and she was as pale as the hospital walls.

"She's going to be fine," Cody said, trying to assure Mrs. Duke. "She just needs to breathe in some more fancy oxygen and rest."

"J.W., we've been just awful to our little girl."

Mr. Duke pulled out a half-chewed cigar from his pocket and put it in his mouth. "You're right."

Mrs. Duke dropped Cody's hand and rubbed the top of Laura's. "We have to be more attuned to what she says."

"We do," J.W. said.

Cody knew what J.W. didn't say—that he'd listen to Laura on some things, but not when it related to Cody Masters or the Double M.

He had to get out of there for a while. Besides, the Dukes deserved some time alone with their daughter.

"I'll be back," he said, then left the room to

search for a steaming cup of coffee so thick that a horseshoe would float in it.

The hospital's cafeteria was the perfect place to go, but he didn't count on seeing the EMT who took care of Laura or the man who was the master of ceremonies during the luncheon on the way there.

"I'm Mark Franco. I'm the manager of the Duke Springs Hotel and Conference Center." He held out his right hand for a shake and brandished a brown leather purse in his left hand. "I think this is Laura Duke's. I believe that you called looking for it."

"I did."

"Everything seems to be in order," Franco said, "But I don't know for sure."

"Good."

"And I'd like to thank you myself. If it weren't for you, Mr. Masters, I shudder to think what the casualties would have been."

Cody shook his head. "Your staff needs training as to how to evacuate, partner. No one showed up early enough, and when they did, they didn't have a clue as to what to do, especially getting out those who use wheelchairs, walkers and others who have difficulty walking."

"I'm aware of that, and action has already been initiated."

"Good." Cody nodded. "I don't want anything to happen again, like it did to Laura."

"Miss Duke is very important to us," Franco said.

And Mr. Duke is very important, too. He probably owns the hotel. You don't want to tick him off and have someone, like his daughter, die in the ladies' room.

Franco looked as if he was about to have a meltdown. "It was a very unfortunate incident. Thank goodness you were there, Mr. Masters. You saved the lives of everyone at that luncheon, and Miss Duke's, as well. How can we thank you? Can we offer you anything?"

Cody didn't want to hear any more praise. He just did what he had to. "A thank-you is enough. Just get your staff trained."

"Consider it done," said Mr. Franco.

Cody followed the smell of coffee to the cafeteria. It was just closing. A metal fence was lowered and women were cleaning up.

Darn!

"Is there just one cup of coffee left?" Cody asked.

"Um…uh…well, we're closed and we're not supposed to—" A young girl with piercings on her nose and lips, purple hair, jeans and a food-spattered white T-shirt with the hospital logo on it seemed ready to give in.

The EMT followed behind him. "Patty, I think you can find a cup of joe for the man who saved three hundred people from a fire, can't you?"

"Sure can!" she said, reaching for a foam cup. "How do you like it?"

"Black."

She handed him the filled cup through the fencing.

"Thanks, Patty." He reached into his pocket for some money.

"Oh, no. It's on me."

Cody smiled. "Thanks again."

"You're a hero," said the EMT.

"Nah." Cody took a sip. The coffee was hot, old, disgusting, and it was the best cup he'd had since prison.

He shook hands with the EMT.

"I'm Ralph Redman. It's a pleasure to know you, Cody."

Cody nodded, uncomfortable with the praise.

"You know, you really are a hero," Redman said before he walked out the door by the cafeteria. "And I know your history…" Redman paused. "I'm going to tell the world what you did tonight. You deserve a lot of credit."

Cody was just about to tell the man not to make a big deal out of it, but he'd already left.

Cody took a deep breath. It was time to go back to Laura's room. Maybe the Dukes would be gone, and he could be alone with her.

But the Dukes weren't gone.

Cody had to hear all about how J.W. phoned for a helicopter, how it landed on a grassy patch on his spread, and in no time at all he was at the hospital in Duke Springs—on the helicopter pad he'd funded—and how he didn't have to deal with overflowing arroyos and flash flooding.

Isn't it nice to be rich?

That was the theme that ran through all of J.W.'s conversations.

All Cody wanted was for them to go so he could hold Laura's hand.

Aw...the hell with it!

As J.W. was talking and chewing on his cigar at the same time and Penny was typing on her cell phone, Cody walked to the side of Laura's hospital bed and took her hand.

J.W. stopped talking.

Penny stopped typing.

Cody still held her hand, leaned down, and whispered to her, "It's Cody, and I'm holding your hand right in front of your parents."

Laura smiled slightly—so slight that only Cody could notice. Shoot! She was awake but faking sleep.

"Sweetheart, you are faking," he whispered. "Open your eyes and show your parents you're okay. Maybe then they'll leave and we can be alone."

She opened her eyes and her parents noticed immediately. They came running to her side.

She lifted her oxygen mask. "I'm fine. Really. They're going to let me out in the morning after a breathing test, but I'm really fine—thanks to Cody. If Cody hadn't found me…" She shuddered. "I owe my life to him."

She was laying it on thick.

"We know that, honey. We will amply reward him," Penny said.

Cody shifted on his feet. "I don't want a reward, ample or otherwise."

"Why don't you take the rest of the week off, Cody," J.W. said.

"That's very generous of you, but no thanks. I'd like to keep up with Johnny's riding lessons."

Dammit. He shouldn't have mentioned Johnny.

Thank goodness Clarissa was in their corner.

"I can't be beholden to you," J.W. said.

"Then let me serve my two years on my own ranch, not yours," Cody said.

Hey, it was worth a try.

J.W. actually seemed to be thinking about it.

"I'll talk to your parole officer. We'll see what we can work out," J.W. reluctantly said.

"That's nice of you, Dad."

"I always pay my debts," he said.

"Just what I want to be—a debt," Laura whispered to Cody. "You should have asked him for my hand in marriage."

"Oh, I will. I will. Someday. When I have a death wish. But I don't want it to be a debt thing," Cody whispered back so only Laura could hear him.

J.W. and Penny stared at them.

"When will you be leaving, Cody?" Penny said to him.

"That's up to Laura."

"I want Cody to stay. Let him stay," she said. "I'll call you in the morning, Mother, and if the roads are dry, you can pick us up. My car is at the hotel."

"Cody, where is your car?" Penny asked, tapping a lacquered finger on the nightstand.

"Oh, Laura drove. She picked me up at the Double M." He told the truth before Laura could make up a lie.

"I see," Penny said. "So you two are sneaking around behind our backs."

"Sneaking?" Cody said. "Yep. We're a pair of sneaks. It's the only way we can see each other. We've been sneaking around for years."

Steam was coming out of J.W.'s ears. Penny was sighing like an actress in a silent movie.

So much for their little truce.

"Where's my grandson?" J.W. growled.

Laura jumped in before Cody could say more. "He's with Clarissa, as usual."

"On her day off?"

"Dad, could you save the interrogation for later? I'm awful tired," Laura said, yawning.

What a great actress, Cody thought. But she'd probably had to be throughout her life.

"I'm glad you're all right, Laura. And I thank you again, Cody, for saving my daughter's life, but I'm not done with the two of you yet," J. W. said.

They both kissed Laura, and then left the room.

"Well, that was fun," Cody said, shaking his head.

"You told them everything," Laura said. "Oh, well. I am tired of lying, too. And my relief is probably due to my recent brush with death, but I'm glad you told them." She squeezed his hand. "I'm wondering if they are going to finally realize that you're a good man and let me date you out in the open, or if they are going to be worse than before."

"You know how I'd bet. It'll be worse than before."

Chapter Eleven

On Sunday, Laura sat in the makeshift bleachers at Skeeter McAvoy's ranch and held her breath while she watched Cody ride practice bulls.

Laura was so nervous that she was biting her fingernails—a habit she broke while in high school. Every time Cody got bucked off, she jumped to her feet, praying that the bull wouldn't step on him or roll him like a log with his horns.

Cody wasn't in top form, not the way he was

when he'd won the Professional Bull Riders World Finals in Las Vegas, but knowing him, he'd try and try until he got his rhythm back.

Since the Duke Ranch Rodeo was starting this weekend, Cody didn't have much more time to practice, if at all. Tomorrow, all the ranch hands would be called upon to get the Duke Ranch's rodeo stock and supplies ready for the fairgrounds where the event would be held. Then they had to transport all the rodeo stock: bucking broncs, steers, bulls and lots of horses.

Stock would come from other area ranches, but the quality stock from the Duke Ranch would be what the cowboys always hoped to draw.

She'd always wanted to put together the annual Duke Ranch Rodeo, but no matter how much she asked, her father always hired a production staff.

Instead, she was regulated to working with

the University of Arizona about how to keep the Duke name off the four-year "scholarship" that the foundation was funding for Slim Gonzalez's son and working with a committee for the new therapy pool for the rehab center.

She could do it all, if only her father would trust her.

She sighed, thinking of how Johnny would love to be here watching Cody ride bulls, but Penny took him to the photographer downtown to have updated pictures taken. Then they were going to have lunch and shop for new sneakers for Johnny.

Johnny made it clear that he wanted new cowboy boots instead of sneaks—boots like Cody's. Laura was sure that Penny would buy him what she wanted instead.

Laura begged off the shopping trip, giving a couple of fake coughs that she hoped sounded authentic. The second her mother pulled out of the driveway, she headed here—to Skeeter McAvoy's ranch off the interstate.

Today she wasn't worried about J.W. He was busy with his rodeo stock at the ranch and shouting orders like a five-star general. She wouldn't be missed.

Cody had the weekend off, or else J.W. would be back to screaming at him, too. Her father had a short memory about who had saved her life.

Smiling, she watched as Cody walked toward her. He had such long legs, and he could certainly work a pair of jeans.

His turquoise-blue eyes were twinkling with happiness and he wore a big grin. Dirt clung to him like a second skin.

"I'm really rusty," Cody said. "I don't know if I have a chance of winning."

"I'm worried about you. You're out of shape for riding bulls, and I don't want you hurt."

He pulled her into his arms and swung her around. "I have until Friday to—"

"Oh, for heaven's sake, Cody, that's only four days away. How many more practice bulls can you get on by then?"

"As many as I can."

"That might not be enough."

He sat down next to her on the splintered bleacher. "Don't be worried. It's the only way I can think of to make some quick money."

"And you'll spend it all on surgeons."

He grinned. "I am so happy to have you in my corner."

"That's not it, Cody. I just don't want you to get hurt."

"There are excellent bull fighters that are going to work the bull riding. Your father contracted the best. I know them and have watched them for years. They'll protect me from getting trampled."

"Cody, they can only do so much."

He chuckled. "That's my woman! She keeps cheering me on and believing in me!"

"Oh, and where do you think J.W. and my mother will be?" He was just about to answer, when she waved her hand. "My mother will be in their box with Johnny and whomever she invites to join her. My father likes to go down to the chutes and pull the rope for the cowboys who draw his bulls. I can just see you drawing a bull from the Duke Ranch and J.W. leaning over the chute, pulling your rope."

Laura grinned at the thought.

"What are you trying to say? You want me to throw the ride if I draw a bull from the Duke Ranch?"

"Don't you dare!" She sighed. "I was just thinking that the Duke Ranch Rodeo will be very interesting this year—kind of like how our lives are going."

He put his arm around her and pulled her tight to him. He stared into her grass-green eyes and raised her lips to his. He kissed Laura, long and hard, then showered her with little kisses and strong hugs.

She was in heaven.

Laura pulled away when a group of loud cowboys distracted her.

"Maybe your father and I should have a side bet," he joked. "If I ride his bull, I'll get his daughter's hand in marriage."

She laughed. "He's a betting man, as you know. Be careful, Cody."

"I'd never bet the Double M, but maybe he'd wager a bull or a top horse."

"And what do you have to offer him?"

He thought for a while, and Laura immediately regretted asking that question.

"I don't have anything," he said.

A group of cowboys walked toward them, laughing, jeering. "Hey, jailbird! We hear you're going to ride bulls at the Duke Rodeo."

"You hear right," Cody said slowly. They

laughed harder, as if it was the best joke they'd ever heard.

"Don't do it," one of the taller and skinnier cowboys said.

"Why's that?"

"Don't throw a punch. We outnumber you."

Cody tensed, and Laura put her hand in his. She could feel every muscle in him tense. He was coiled and ready to spring.

"Just ignore them," Laura said.

Another one of the group spit in the dirt at Cody's feet. "It's a family event, Masters. We don't like riding with murderers."

"I've done my time," Cody said calmly.

"You have beans in your ears? We don't like killers, pal. Rodeo is a family sport."

"What are you worried about? That I'll win?" Cody asked. "If you've been watching me ride, you'll know that I don't have much of a shot, so don't worry."

That made them laugh and suddenly they were all pals.

After handshakes and introductions, the group walked away.

Men! Sheesh!

When they were out of earshot, Cody kicked at a stone with his boot. "I never thought about my record. I just never gave it a thought. All I could think of was that I'm entering as a former champ. I never thought about the reaction of the riders and probably the spectators."

He took his hat off and slapped it on his thigh. "Dammit, Laura! How much more can I take?"

"That's it, Johnny. Keep your legs down so you won't bounce around. And keep your feet in the stirrups. Go around the corral until I tell you to reverse. Then when it's time for reverse, I want you to move the reins against Pirate's neck like I showed you—move them in the direction that you want to go. Got it?"

"Got it!"

Cody followed the horse and rider closely, but then eventually gave Johnny more space.

"Reverse," Cody said, and Johnny did as he was told. Pirate obeyed. "Perfect!"

"Am I ready for a trail ride with you and Momma?"

"Not yet, but soon. I have more to show you."

"Ride 'em, cowboy!" J.W. yelled from the barn ramp that led to the corral. "Nice job!"

"Grandpa, I'm riding really good."

"You sure are, buckaroo." J.W. then turned his attention to Cody. "Cody, I'd like to see you."

"I'll be with you right after Johnny's lesson."

J.W. motioned for Cody to come to him. "We can talk right here. This won't take long."

"Walk Pirate around the corral, Johnny. Nothing fancy."

Cody watched to make sure his son was doing as instructed. He sure hoped that J.W.

was going to let him work at the Double M instead of here.

"Yes?" he asked.

"I spoke with your parole officer, and we are going to let you work two weekdays at your own ranch, but you have to continue with Johnny's half-hour lesson every weekday here. And I'd like to offer you a position at the B barn, training Arabians for certain special clients."

That was a dream job. Trainers didn't have to shovel manure.

J.W. grunted. "This isn't because I give a sh—"

Just then, Pirate walked by with Johnny. He looked serious and was concentrating on not letting his legs and feet bounce.

"Great job, Johnny. Great job!" J.W. said once the boy was past them. "This isn't because I give a crap about you, Masters. It's because you saved my daughter's life and I always pay my debts. I can't have everyone find out that I have a damn hero mucking out stalls."

"Hero? *What?*" Cody asked.

J.W. ignored him. "I'm giving you those terms. Take them or leave them."

"I'll take them," Cody said. "If I can ride in your rodeo—the bull riding event. I'm scheduled to work this Friday, and as you know, it's a three-day event, and—"

"As far as I know, you haven't ridden anything for years. Have your lost your mind?"

"Maybe, but it would give me a lot of pleasure to take your money," Cody said.

He thought he saw J.W. attempt a smile.

"I don't like a convict riding in my rodeo, but suit yourself. It might make good publicity for the rodeo. Right next to the front-page article about you saving three hundred people from a fire."

J.W. pulled a rolled-up newspaper from the back pocket of his jeans and tossed it to

Cody, then walked away. "Watch my grandson closely, Masters."

"Of course."

After Pirate was brushed and his tack was cleaned, Cody walked Johnny back to the ranch house. Laura was there to greet them with lemonade and cookies, only because Penny was in town and J.W. had left.

"I probably should get back to work, Laura."

"Stay and have some refreshments with us. I'll protect you." She laughed.

Cody grinned and asked Johnny, "Want to sit on my lap? You can reach the table better."

"'Kay."

Cody hoisted him up and they munched on sugar cookies and sipped lemonade, although Cody was sure that his jeans were wet from Johnny's lemonade spills in certain unmentionable areas.

They talked, laughed and joked and Cody knew just what he'd been missing all those years. This was what it felt like to have a family of his own, to sit at a table with his wife and son and really enjoy himself by just being with them.

So much time lost.

"Johnny, do you want to go with me to the rodeo and watch Mr. Masters ride bulls?" Laura asked.

"Oh, yeah! How cool!" he said, nodding eagerly. "Can I have some cotton candy? And some popcorn?"

Cody laughed and was about to say "sure," when Laura said, "We'll see."

That was the standard buzzkill from a parent. Well, he was a parent, too. "Sure you can! Sounds good."

When Laura glared at him, he shrugged. "It's a rodeo."

"Are you gonna win, Cody? Are you?"

"That's Mr. Masters, sweetie," Laura corrected.

The boy shrugged. "That's what I meant, Mom. Cody. Mr. Masters. It's the same guy."

"He has a point there, Laura. I'm the same guy."

But how I wish he could call me Dad.

"Laura, how much longer?" he asked, knowing that she'd know exactly what he meant.

"I don't know, Cody. Don't rush me. I'll know when the time is right."

"Huh?" Johnny asked.

"Nothing, cowboy." Reluctantly, Cody lifted him and set him on his feet. "I have to get back to work. Those stalls aren't going to muck themselves out, and then I'm done with mucking. I'm training horses, starting tomorrow."

Laura grinned. He figured that she'd put a bug in her father's ear.

"See you tomorrow, Johnny. Tomorrow I'm going to teach you how to trot. You'll do that for a couple of days. How's that?"

Cody waited for the word he knew Johnny would say: "Cool."

"Oh, I forgot about this." Cody picked up the *Springs Gazette* that he'd put down on the table. The headline read Ex-Convict Turns Hero. Immediately, Cody didn't want to read further.

"Read it out loud, Cody," Laura said. "I already read it, but I want to hear it again. And Johnny should hear it—some of it, not all."

"Nah, I don't think so."

"Then give it to me," Laura said. Taking the paper from the table, she began to read, "'Acting without concern for himself, Cody Masters, of the Double M Ranch in Duke Springs, evacuated approximately three hundred individuals who were at a conference at the Duke Springs Hotel and Conference Center when a fire broke out in the kitchen.

"'In a twist of fate right out of the movies, one of the victims he saved from smoke inhalation and certain death was none other than the guest speaker, Laura Duke of Duke Ranch, whom Masters found passed out on the floor in the ladies' room.'

"Oh, for heaven's sake, did they have to mention ladies' room?" Laura asked. "And it sounds like I was drinking. Passed out. Sheesh."

"'Masters, who was recently released from—'" Laura sniffed. "I think I'll skip that. It's the boring part," she said to Johnny.

"'Many of the victims were in wheelchairs, and hotel staff was slow to respond. When they finally did, Masters had the situation under control.

"'Cody Masters is a hero who saved the day. If there is a reason for someone's past to be forgotten, it's the fire at the Springs Hotel. Cody Masters has proved himself to this community.

"'When you see Cody Masters on the street, shake his hand and thank him for saving your friends, neighbors, relatives and loved ones.'

"Cody, that's really nice." Laura leaned over

and gave him a chaste kiss on the cheek. "You were always a hero to me."

"Momma, did you just kiss Cody?" Johnny asked.

"I did, sweetie. Cody saved my life."

"Yeah." Johnny held out his hand to Cody, and they shook. "Thanks for saving my mom."

"You're welcome, partner."

Cody's eyes were misty as he turned away.

Cody told Slim that he was picking Thursdays and Fridays to work at the Double M. Thursday, he'd get on as many practice bulls as he could. Friday night was the first round of the bull-riding competition.

The competition continued on Saturday night and Sunday noon, with the short go-round on Sunday.

Excellent money could be won all three days, and Cody was as ready as he could be. Skeeter McAvoy had let him ride every bull in his practice pen at least twice, and with Skeeter's help, Cody had definitely improved.

On Thursday night, he set up an empty fifty-gallon drum in his barn and strung it up on bungee cords. He practiced on the barrel until he mastered that.

Throughout the week, he did a lot of core exercises and curls. He was in the best physical shape he could be after those years in prison. He'd never missed an opportunity to exercise.

He was as ready as he would ever be.

On Friday morning, as he was practicing on the barrel at the Double M, Laura and Johnny came for a visit.

"Everyone's gone to the fairgrounds to get things rolling and the stock settled. Mom is at a fashion show for breast cancer research, but I told her that I couldn't come because I wanted to let Johnny go on the rides. Would you like to join us?"

He looked at Johnny's smiling face. "I'd love

to, but first I have to give Johnny his riding lesson and do some things around here."

"Johnny, tell Mr. Masters what we discussed."

"That I don't have to ride Pirate today. I can
go on the rides instead and have popcorn and
cotton candy," he said.

Cody snapped his fingers. "Johnny, how
would you like to go mutton bustin' at the
rodeo? You ride on woolly sheep."

"Cool."

"Um… I don't know about that," Laura said.
"I don't want him hurt."

"You know that I wouldn't do anything to
put Johnny in harm's way," Cody said quietly,
evenly. "He's not going to get hurt. The event
is controlled and watched carefully. The kids
wear helmets and vests."

"Just like you when you ride bulls?" Johnny
asked.

"Just like me." Matter of fact, Cody remembered that he needed to find his old vest and

chaps and see if they'd fit him for the event tonight. He was old-school and rode without a helmet, but he should have found the time to buy one.

J.W. had a pen of crazy bulls.

"You two discuss it. Maybe discuss it with J.W. I think he'd love to see Johnny do some mutton bustin'."

Laura turned to Johnny. "Honey, let's go back home and you can put on your new cowboy boots and your new hat. You have to look like a cowboy when you go mutton bustin'."

"Yes! Yee-haw!" Johnny yelled, then ran like crazy back to their truck.

"Since when do you care what J.W. thinks?" Laura asked when Johnny was out of earshot.

"I don't care what he thinks." Cody shrugged. "And I honestly don't know why I said that."

Laura pointed to his makeshift bull and laughed. "Your brains are rattled."

"Yeah, maybe. But maybe someone needs to

hold out the olive branch in peace—so we can be a family."

For the first time in a long time, Laura was speechless, then said, "I've never known a time when the Masters and Dukes haven't fought. It's all over a strip of land."

They stood in silence, thinking.

"No, Laura, my fight with J.W. is over you."

"True." Laura sighed. "And my mother and yours have a bad history. It's about time they buried that, too. I don't think my mother has been very happy throughout the years, and certainly yours wasn't happy with Lindy."

"We have to remove ourselves from their mess and make a family of our own," Cody said. "I've never been so determined to win money riding bulls. This means more to me than when I won the world championship."

"Come to think of it, where is all that money you won, Cody? You won thousands and thousands of dollars."

"I put it back into the ranch. We bought some stock, fixed up some things. Bought a shiny red pickup that's now that pink wreck that we drive. Put in a new septic system and got water to the barn. And then it was gone. It didn't last long."

Laura checked her watch. "You go ahead and do what you have to. I'll meet you at the kids' rides. Johnny will have cotton candy all over his face, and I'll be the one sticky from holding his hand. Then later, we'll enter the mutton bustin'."

"And then cheer for me, Laura. Cheer for *us*. We have our whole lives resting on my riding. If I win enough, we can get that brand-new double-wide and put it on the Double M property."

Laura smiled, and gave Cody a hug and a big kiss. "I'll be cheering for you, Cody. You know I will. See you later. And in case I forget to tell you, we'll be sitting in the box seats to the left of the chutes in the arena."

Even though Laura was saying the right things, her kiss was cold, and Cody wondered what was wrong now.

Chapter Twelve

"I want to go on the caterpillar," Johnny said.

Laura peeled off a ticket and handed it to the kid running the ride—a tame, roller coaster shaped like a caterpillar's body.

"Go for it," she said as he ran to the back of the line.

"He needs some kids his own age to play with," Cody said as they sat on a bench by the ride. "How come he doesn't have any friends?"

"He's not in school yet. He goes in two months—in September. Kindergarten."

"Oh yeah."

"He does have playdates with some kids from church, but I don't see them here yet."

"Okay."

They sat looking at Johnny standing in line, talking to a little girl behind him. He had on his cowboy hat, a long-sleeved shirt, jeans and boots, and he looked darn cute, waiting for his turn.

"He's a good kid, Laura. You did a fine job."

"So did my parents, Cody. I know you don't want to hear that, but they're great with him. Your mother adores him, too, and Cindy, of course."

"Thanks for bringing him to the Double M, and letting him know my mom and sis. I can't wait until we tell Johnny that my mother is his grandmother and Cindy is his aunt."

Laura shifted on the bench, looking uncomfortable, but Cody didn't want to broach a touchy subject. This was a day for fun.

"Laura, after this ride and maybe another, we need to get going to the arena and register Johnny for the mutton bustin'."

"He's been so excited. He thinks he's a bull rider, like you."

"Better that he should pass out money, like you."

"Laura Duke! For heaven's sake, I've been trying to contact you." A statuesque woman with designer jeans and a cherry-red sequined jacket that sparkled in the afternoon sun stood in front of them. Cody would bet that she was a former Miss Arizona Rodeo.

Laura nodded to the woman. "Cody, this is Cricket Adams. She's on the school board with me and we're on a couple of other committees together."

Cody held out his hand to shake hers, and she looked down at him as if snakes were crawling out of his ears.

He lowered his hand.

Laura didn't miss the snub and immediately became defensive. "What did you call about, Cricket?"

"There was an emergency meeting of the executive committee of the school board. It was decided that your talents are best served elsewhere," she said. "I volunteered to tell you the news."

"I don't understand, Cricket," Laura said. "Why the emergency meeting? What's really going on?"

"It was felt that your, um…choice of acquaintances does not reflect positively on you." She looked down her nose at Cody. "That school board members should set a good example for our youth, and you aren't doing that by being seen with a…a…"

"I believe the word you are looking for is *murderer*, Cricket," Cody said.

She grasped the gold chains at her neck. "How rude!"

Cody picked up Laura's hand. "I think you've cornered the market on rudeness. So has the school board."

Laura sat stunned until Cody squeezed her hand, and finally she gathered herself enough to speak. "It is none of the board's business who my friends are. Cody did his time, paid his debt and saved three hundred people from a fire. I'm sure you know that."

Laura stood, dismissing her. "Excuse me, Cricket. My son is done with the caterpillar, and we have time for another ride before he goes mutton bustin'. Please give the school board my best."

Cody turned to Laura and winked. "Geez, Laura, weren't you just going to give each of the school board members a cruise to the Bahamas as a gift for their service? That's too bad that you won't be there anymore to do that." He shrugged. "Well, let's go get Johnny. The ride is over."

Cody followed her to the ride, and when he looked back at the glittering Cricket, her mouth was hanging open, and she was frozen in position. Then a little girl holding a fresh cone of pink cotton candy bumped into her. Cricket squealed and began picking the stuff out of her sequins.

He nudged Laura and pointed to Cricket. "Sometimes you get what you deserve."

But Laura didn't laugh. She had tears in her eyes.

The mutton bustin' cheered her up. The kids couldn't have been cuter, clinging to their furry sheep as if they were stuck on them like burdock.

"Johnny's age group is up next," Cody said, leaning on the wooden fence.

Laura grabbed his hand, squeezing it hard. She'd told her parents earlier about Johnny's event, and Cody could see them in their private box, on their feet, cameras at the ready.

He had to give them credit. They adored Johnny.

Georgianna and Cindy had made it to the first row of cheap seats, one flight up. Not bad seats; nothing like what the Dukes had, but they adored Johnny, too.

Johnny won third prize for staying on his sheep. The poor little guy started to cry when he was told that he wouldn't get another turn because his age group was completed. He wanted to ride again.

Cody glanced over at J.W., and it looked as if he was going to have Johnny ride again. Laura caught his eye and mouthed the word *no*.

"Good call, Laura. Johnny has to learn that he can't have everything, unlike your father."

"My father worked for everything he has, Cody."

"Haven't we all?" Cody asked.

"Yes. Yes, we have. You're right."

* * *

Laura just wasn't the same. Up until Cricket came chirping about the school board, Laura had been happier than he'd seen her in a while.

"If you stick with me, Laura, you're always going to be guilty by association. And there're always going to be people like Cricket. It won't matter what wonderful things you've done before or are currently involved in."

"I'm beginning to realize that. I mean, I thought of it before, but only in terms of Johnny having a father who is a convicted murderer. I think I can take it, but Johnny will have it tough throughout his whole life."

There was silence between them as they walked to claim Johnny. No wonder Laura was hesitant to tell her parents and his mother about him being Johnny's father. She didn't want Johnny to bear the weight of his father being a convict in small-town Duke Springs.

As far as Cody was concerned, children could almost be as cruel as adults.

"So you don't want to tell your parents or my family that I'm Johnny's father because of how my murder conviction would trickle down to you and Johnny. That's correct, isn't it, Laura? That's why you don't want to marry me, and with your job, you can somewhat control the people of Duke Springs. You wield a lot of power with the fund."

"And I wouldn't hesitate to use it. In that way, I'm like my parents," she snapped.

Cody shook his head. "And I can save hundreds of people from a fire, but I can never wipe my slate clean, can I?"

"No. You can never do that."

"I think that Cricket did me a favor." He whistled long and low. "And to think that I was going to risk my neck riding bulls for us, but that's only money, and it isn't going to get to the heart of our problem, is it?"

She didn't say a word, but there were tears in her eyes.

"And the truth is that you'll always be ashamed of being with me. So will Johnny. After all these years, we just don't know each other, do we?"

"Cody, I—"

Johnny was approaching, swinging his ribbon. He was finally smiling, so someone had had a talk with him. And here he was ready to give his son a discussion about how there was no crying in rodeo!

Johnny didn't need him.

Laura didn't need him.

"I have to go," he said. "I've decided to ride bulls, after all. I can't think of a better way to take out my frustration." He tweaked the brim of his hat. "Goodbye."

"Cody, I'm so sorry. I—"

"Goodbye. Tell Johnny I'll see him tomorrow for his riding lesson. And, Laura, maybe you should listen to everyone and stay away from me."

Laura felt miserable. It was as if she'd betrayed and hurt her best friend.

Cody had guessed the reason why she didn't want to get married—not yet, anyway. It was bad enough that Cody was a community pariah, but why should she and Johnny suffer the same fate?

Just how shallow can I be?

So now it was out in the open.

Was she ashamed of being seen with him? Maybe. Sometimes. But not when she could control the situation, like the church picnic. With him bidding on her box lunch, she had an excuse to be with him in public.

She had just experienced firsthand how awful people could be.

Could she handle getting kicked off of her various committees?

She probably could, but hated the thought. As head of the Duke Foundation, she wielded a lot of power, but even that and money didn't protect her from being kicked off the school board.

And, most important, there was Johnny to consider. His hand was in hers as they walked, and he was holding his third-place ribbon as if it were a bridal bouquet.

Johnny was just so cute and kind to everyone he met. It was hard enough being a kid, without having a felon for a father.

She didn't want the kids to taunt him.

She didn't want her son hurt in any way.

Cody had become distant after the Cricket disaster. He was ticked at her, and hurt, and deservedly so.

But maybe Cody should try to understand where she was coming from.

Oh, he probably did.

As they waited in line for cotton candy, Laura decided that she'd give Cody a couple of days to cool off and then they'd talk.

Does absence really make the heart grow fonder? Or does it just postpone the inevitable?

And just what was the inevitable?

Was their love going to survive the sinkhole that was threatening to suck them both in, or would it be stronger than before?

Cody saw Laura and Johnny in the Duke Ranch boxed seats. Johnny's face and hands were deep into the cotton candy of his dreams—blue.

J.W. and Penny weren't there yet.

Laura and Johnny couldn't see Cody watching them behind the chutes near a curtain that led to the locker room. As he watched them, he wondered if they'd ever become a family.

"So, are you going to win this thing, Masters?" It was J. W. Duke himself. Cody was so deep in his thoughts, he hadn't even seen J.W. walking toward him.

"I sure as hell am going to try."

"How about a small wager?" J.W. asked, chewing on the stub of a cigar.

"No. I'm not going to put up our land, our home, our barn or our stock. But I wouldn't mind if you put up Cowabunga. If I win, I get him. And he's a beauty. Good breeding stock."

The shifting of the cigar stub in his mouth led Cody to believe that J.W. was actually thinking about it.

"Okay. If you win this thing on Sunday, you get Cowabunga. If you lose, you owe me thirty days without pay."

"I can't afford to lose a month of pay," Cody said.

"Then you're not as confident as you seem to be."

"Confident?" Cody grunted. "I must be a good actor."

"You're a better magician, always showing up at places where Laura is, even when I ordered you not to go near her."

"Did you ever think that she turns up at places where I am?"

"Do *you* think I built an empire by being stupid?" J.W. asked.

Cody bit back a grin. "I'll take the thirty days without pay, but I can't do it in a lump. If I lose, I'll have to spread it out."

J.W. nodded and held out his hand. Cody didn't hesitate, but returned the handshake. This wasn't being friendly—J.W. was hardly his friend. It was a business agreement.

"I'd better see if my chaps fit. And my vest. And I have to see if anyone will lend a helmet to an ex-con."

"Good luck with that."

Cody nodded and ducked into the locker

room. Looking back, he saw J.W. walk around greeting everyone and shaking hands as if he were campaigning to be president of the United States. Then Cody took a last look at Laura and Johnny in the bleachers.

He couldn't believe that Laura was ashamed of him. He'd told her that he was innocent, and she believed him, but the stigma of his conviction would never be erased. He could understand her reasoning, but where did that leave him? He couldn't imagine not being with her or Johnny.

He was still going to ride for them. If nothing else, he'd give Laura the money to put toward college for Johnny, and in the meantime, he was still going to give Johnny a riding lesson every day.

But as he told Laura, maybe she needed some time alone to work things out in her mind.

Until then, he was going to cowboy up.

* * *

Cody was up next, and Laura could barely breathe. Johnny was jumping out of his skin waiting for "Mr. Masters to ride Cowabunga."

Johnny liked saying *Cowabunga*. He must have repeated it a hundred times. Cowabunga was a very sweet two-thousand-pound Brahma with horns on his head that were so thick and big they looked like two baseball bats.

Cowabunga would let Johnny pet him, but when he had a rider on his back...watch out!

As the camera followed him to the chutes and they broadcasted every move Cody made on the big screen in the middle of the arena, Cody looked every inch the cowboy. He wore a black hat, a nice pastel-plaid long-sleeved shirt and jeans, of course. His old chaps, black with red fringe, looked good on him, too.

Laura wished she could tell Cody that she was wrong. That she didn't mean what she'd said, but she couldn't do that.

She did mean it.

The cowboy had saved her life, and she was worried about her reputation.

Something was wrong with her. This was *her* Cody.

Yeah, her Cody with a criminal record.

He nodded and the chute gate opened. Cowabunga burst out as if he had been shot out of a cannon.

Cody hung on. *One second.*

He was getting off balance as Cowabunga kicked up his back legs and spun into circles at the same time. *Three seconds. Four seconds.*

Cody was able to get back to the center of the bull. *Five seconds. Six seconds.*

Laura stood up and so did Johnny. "You can do it, Cody. Ride. Ride!"

"C'mon, Mr. Masters," Johnny echoed.

He was getting off center again. *Seven seconds.*

Cody was hanging precariously off the side of

the bull, his face near the bull's sharp, stomping hooves.

She held her breath. "Careful, Cody. Careful!"

Eight seconds!

He did it!

"Johnny, he did it!" They hugged and Laura picked up Johnny and swung him in a circle. "And he's okay."

Laura looked at the people around her. The usually boisterous crowd was unusually quiet, but a good portion of them clapped and cheered, drowning out the boos.

She sat down and patted the chair next to her for Johnny to sit.

Her face flamed. How ridiculous. Why did the crowd bother her? The truth was, she cared about what people thought. And she cared about what they thought about Cody.

She turned around and found Georgianna

and Cindy and gave them a thumbs-up. They did the same in return.

Out of the thirty riders, Cody came in third in points. He had to do better on his second bull.

He did, and he moved up to second place.

Then he won the short go—the final round of the top fifteen best riders—and won the event for that day.

Cody rode a total of three bulls, and would receive twenty-one thousand dollars.

Laura was so happy for him, but then it came time for the presentation of the gold buckle in the middle of the arena. Again, there were some boos, not only from the crowd, but from some of the other riders, as well.

She could see Cody's face flame, and she felt sick to her stomach. This should be a triumph for him, but instead it was a negative experience.

Like a true cowboy, Cody tipped his hat to the crowd, then disappeared quickly.

At eleven o'clock the next morning, Cody met Johnny and Laura at the main Duke barn for Johnny's lesson. He had to get to the rodeo arena soon after.

"Hey, Mr. Masters! You won! You sure can ride those bulls."

"Thanks, Johnny. I appreciate it."

"Can you teach me how to ride bulls like you?"

"Someday. When you're older and if your mom says it's okay."

"She won't."

Cody laughed. "You're probably right. Now let me watch you walk Pirate around the corral by yourself. I'll tell you when to stop and go. Then we'll brush Pirate and clean the tack."

His cell phone rang just after the lesson as he was getting some water for the horse. "Hi, Mom. What's up?"

"Cody, you have to call a number that I'll text to you. It's important."

"What's it about?"

"You'll see. I don't want to spoil it for you."

Cody's interest was piqued. "Okay, I'll call them back."

"Make sure you do. And then call me right back."

It turned out to be the sheriff's department.

"Dammit! What the hell did I do now?" he said under his breath.

Lieutenant Foxworth was very complimentary. "Cody Masters, you've been nominated by the Duke Springs Citizens' Committee to receive our Person of the Year award in the safety category for evacuating the crowd at the hotel. The committee wishes to honor you at a dinner and awards night. We will pay for you and a guest. If you wish to bring more guests, I can get you tickets at half price. The more the merrier, Mr. Masters."

"Person of the Year?"

"Yes. We have different categories—safety, community service, law enforcement, volunteer—that kind of thing. As I mentioned, you are getting the safety award."

"I'm honored, sir, but I'm going to pass. I don't need an award in recognition of doing the right thing. Besides, some of the good people of Duke Springs just booed me at the rodeo, so it would be ludicrous to accept their award. Thanks anyway, Lieutenant."

Cody hung up the phone. Even good news made him miserable.

Chapter Thirteen

"The sheriff's department wants to give Cody an award?" Laura asked, intrigued.

"Yeah. Doesn't that beat all?" In his office in the ranch house, J.W. leafed through a bunch of invoices and whatnot, barely paying attention to her.

He looked up at her. "And he turned it down. He said he was booed at the rodeo. Said the people wouldn't want him to get that award."

"He was. You were there. You must have heard. Wasn't it awful?" she asked.

He shrugged.

"Oh, forget it, Dad. You were probably one of the ones booing him." When he didn't respond, she said, "I'm going to go downtown. Johnny is with Cody for his riding lesson. I think they are done now, though. Then Clarissa will watch him for about an hour or so until I get back."

"Okay."

"Okay. See you later."

"I'm thinking of sending Johnny to nursery school during August. Maybe it'll make it easier for him to transition to kindergarten. And he'll make some friends," Laura said.

"Johnny has everything that a boy could want right here."

"Except friends his own age."

"Well, invite some kids over for him to play with."

"I know!" Laura said. "Let's have a little gathering for the ranch hands and their kids. We can barbecue some hot dogs and hamburgers and whip up some salads. We can have strawberry shortcake for dessert. I'll rent a bounce house. The kids will love jumping around on that. And I'll invite some of my friends from the committees that I work on. They all have children."

"Sounds like a plan. Are you going to handle it, or are you going to get a party planner?"

"I'll handle it."

"Do you think you can?"

"Oh, for heaven's sake. Of course I can!" she said. Then took a couple of deep breaths. "Dad?"

He looked up from his papers. "Yes?"

"I think it's sad the way the people of Duke Springs booed Cody at the rodeo, but he showed them. He won the event last night. Rode all three bulls."

Laura saw a bit of a smile on J.W.'s face. "He sure did. That man can ride."

To her knowledge, J.W. had never said that before.

"See you later, Dad."

She found her keys at the bottom of her purse and drove to the Masters ranch. She just had to drive up the hill that led to her father's house, go to the corner and turn left.

Laura felt bad that she had to lie about where she was going, but that was pretty much the story of her life.

She wanted to talk to Georgianna and Cindy.

The door to the ranch house swung open, and they both came onto the front porch, waving to her as she pulled in to park.

She always felt special whenever she came here. They treated her with such affection that she felt safe and secure here, like family.

But today something was different. They seemed overly welcoming.

"Cody finally told us that you confirmed that Johnny is his son," Georgianna said as they all rocked on the porch. "But we both guessed it ages ago. Cindy was the one who finally pointed Cody in the right direction, showed him a picture when he was Johnny's age."

"I'm glad that the secret is finally out," Laura said.

Some secret. She wondered if her parents suspected anything, but they seemed to have dropped the subject of finding the whereabouts of her college love—at least for now.

"Is something going on between you and Cody?" Georgianna said. "Cody isn't himself, and I'm worried about him. He's riding again tonight, and he needs to concentrate on that and not be distracted."

Much to her dismay, Laura started to cry. "Cody thinks that I'm ashamed of him, but I'm not, not exactly. He's a good man, Georgianna, but with the manslaughter charge and being an ex-con, he's branded, and a lot of people can't understand that he did his time. He paid his debt. I'm tainted by association. Johnny will be, too, when the word gets out that he's Cody's son, because he's the son of a killer," she sniffed. "And it's all a big mess."

Georgianna burst into tears, too. They both dabbed at their eyes and sat in silence for a while, rocking.

Georgianna took Laura's hand. "Trust Cody, Laura."

"It can be hard."

"If you really love him, trust him," Georgianna said. "Excuse me, please."

Laura could hear Georgianna crying, but the sound faded as she went farther into the ranch house.

That left Laura with Cindy. Laura stared at the mountains in the distance.

Cindy put her arm around Laura. "I'd like to say that it'll be okay, but I don't see how, unless the three of us can figure out something. First, I think Cody needs to be convinced to show up at that awards night. He is a hero in more ways than one, and this foolish town needs to realize that."

"How'd you get so smart at age thirteen?" Laura asked.

"I'm going to be fourteen next month."

"I see." Laura bit back a smile. "My father told me about the award, and I agree with you, Cindy. But he's one stubborn cowboy. How can we convince him to go?"

"We? Oh, no. He won't listen to us, but he might listen to you. You're the one whose life he saved—yours and the other two hundred and ninety-nine people."

Laura nodded. "I'll do my best, and I'll make some calls, too."

She prayed that Cody would be at their secret place tonight so she could talk to him, but she doubted it. She'd hurt him horribly.

Maybe the two of them could come up with

some kind of agreement. Maybe he'd accept her apology.

She didn't want to hurt him any more than she already had. She would always love him, but for all of their sakes, it might make more sense to let him go.

Just before the Saturday night bull riding, Cody sat in the spectator bleachers by the chutes, instead of talking to the other cowboys in the locker room.

He was going to blow if he heard one more joke or one more snotty remark about his conviction. So, instead of fighting with them, he walked away and sat in the stands before the doors opened to the public, thinking.

He was ready to ride. He drew Maximilian, a bull that was known for being temperamental and mean, but Cody could be ninety points on him if he could just stay on for eight seconds.

He closed his eyes, picturing the perfect ride,

but scenes of Laura and Johnny intruded instead. They were welcome intrusions, but he couldn't think of any solution to all their problems, except for one big juicy solution, and he wasn't willing to do that—at least not yet. But if things didn't work out, he'd split.

Eventually, the large wooden doors to the arena opened and people trickled in.

Laura walked to the Duke Ranch box seats with Johnny and her parents. Just as soon as he sat down and looked around, Johnny yelled and waved to Georgianna and Cindy.

Laura turned around, as did the Dukes. Penny and J.W. seemed shocked, probably to learn that Johnny knew them. Laura tried to turn Johnny around and get him in his seat, but he insisted on greeting them.

About now, Cody could care less who found out what, and he was going to tell that to Laura in no uncertain terms. If she didn't want to be with him because it would reflect on her reputation, that was fine. But now that he knew that Johnny was his, he was going to be part of the boy's life. A couple hours a day teaching him how to ride just wasn't enough. He wanted to get involved in Johnny's life and play catch with him, help him with his homework, throw him a birthday party...the whole enchilada. He wanted to be the same kind of father that he'd had.

If it came to a family court battle for custody, he had no doubt that he would lose, so he had to be careful. He couldn't afford to tick anyone off.

He thought about his ride again. In a lot of ways it was easier riding a ton of Brahma bull than figuring out his life.

All he knew was that he had to make some changes, and most of them had to do with the Dukes.

He smiled. He sure wanted to win more of J.W.'s money. He got up and went to find Maximilian. He was going to have a long talk with the bull.

"Hey, Masters, Steven Lindy wants to talk to you," said a cowboy standing by a door that led to the back of the arena. A security officer was supposed to be assigned there, but he was gone.

Cody's stomach turned. That's all he needed, a confrontation with Hank Lindy's son.

"Hurry up, Masters, I don't have all day," said the cowboy.

Cody took a deep breath and walked over to the door. Before he had a chance to blink, he was pulled down the stairs by his shirt and a fist crashed into his teeth.

"I've been waiting to get you alone, Masters. That's for killing my father."

Cody swung back, connecting with Steven's chin. Then his arms were pulled behind him and held tightly, straining his shoulders.

"What do you want, Lindy? If you want to

fight me, let's get on with it. Don't talk me to death. And to make this fair, get rid of your lackey."

"I don't want to make this fair. I want to hurt you something awful."

"Uh, I figured that out."

"Why did you do it?"

"You know why," Cody said. "Don't you? I'm sure you could see my mother's bruises in court. And then there was my sister, well…"

He didn't want to rehash the whole thing, although Steven deserved to know the whole story…or maybe he didn't. From what Cody heard after the fact, Hank Lindy wasn't the father of the year, either. Steven had had a tough life with Lindy.

"I don't want to fight you. And I don't want to fight a guy I don't even know."

"My name's Dave," said the lackey.

"I'd shake your hand if you'd let go of my

arms. They're starting to hurt, Dave, and I need both of them to ride."

"Shut the hell up, Masters. I want to think," Steven said.

"Don't strain yourself." Cody admonished himself for egging him on, but he'd learned in prison that if he kept things light, he could get out of a lot of fights.

Steven wound up and socked him in the gut. Cody doubled over in pain and was able to break away from Dave and free his arms.

"Steven, c'mon. I don't want to fight you. And I'm sorry about your father."

The hell I'm sorry.

Cody stopped a right hook to his jaw, but set his diaphragm to absorb the punches to his ribs and chest.

The two of them were on him, but he gave enough warning to Steven before he apologized, although Cody knew that his apology was hollow and it wouldn't bring the man's father back. But what more could he say?

"I did my time, Steven. It was hell, but I did the time. Shouldn't that count for something?"

"Three lousy years? That's it?"

"I did what they gave me."

Cody fended off a couple more punches, but one lucky blow from Dave had him hurting like hell whenever he breathed. He had at least one broken rib, dammit.

Cody sprang into action and hauled off and gave Steven a couple of gut punches. He pivoted and did the same to Dave.

They were coughing and gasping for air. Steven was curled up on the ground like a boiled shrimp.

Cody found it hard to breathe, too.

Cody dusted himself off and wiped his face with a bandanna. There was blood. Lots of blood. He must be cut above his eye. He always bled like crazy from a wound like that. One of them must have been wearing a ring.

"That's all the fun I can take, guys. I have to go and ride bulls now," Cody said, walking away. The door was open, and now there was a security guard stationed there.

"Thanks for nothing, pal," Cody said.

The guard patted his pocket, and Cody could see a bunch of bills folded in half through the material.

Cody grunted and on the way back to his seat in the arena, he came face-to-face with the sports physician. "Come with me to the training room. You need a couple of stitches in your eyebrow, and from the way you're breathing, sounds like you need your ribs taped."

"Nah, I'm okay."

"You're not okay. Let's go."

Cody liked the doctor immediately, so he went with him. He was going to have a couple of black eyes, along with stitches on his eyebrow. His knuckles were raw and bleeding, and the doc sprayed them with some kind of stuff and wrapped them in gauze.

"You can ride with the gauze on. Now, take your shirt off and I'll wrap your ribs."

That was how Laura found him when she walked into the room—sitting on an exam table with taped ribs.

"Cody, what happened?"

"A dissatisfied spectator. He had money bet on me, and I didn't come in high enough for him."

"But you won the round last night!"

"I think he'd bet on the guy who came in second to come in first."

She raised an eyebrow, and gave him "the look" that he knew meant she didn't believe him. He never could fool her.

"You look so awful."

"I'm being complimented by you all the time. It's going to go to my head."

"You know what I mean. What really happened?"

"It was Hank Lindy's son, and a pal of his."

"Oh."

"Steven wanted to rough me up for killing his father." Cody shrugged. "I can't blame him."

"He probably wanted to do more than rough you up," she said.

She touched the tape on his ribs and he could swear that he felt the warmth of her hand through the thickness of the bandage.

Then she gently touched his cheek. It was sore, and he was glad that his jaw wasn't broken, but her touch made him shiver.

"Oh, Cody! I'm so sorry. I'm hurting you."

"No, you're not. It feels good."

"I don't think you should ride with stitches, broken ribs, sore knuckles, a sore jaw and whatever else you have. I worry about you when you're healthy and ready to ride, but now you're hurt, and I can't stand it. Hang up your spurs, Cody."

"Laura, what are you doing here?"

"What do you mean?"

"I thought you were embarrassed to be with me."

She shrugged. "Let's not get into this today. Not when you're riding and aren't up to par."

This was turning out to be one hell of a day.

"Are you still going to ride?" she asked.

"Yup. And I'm going to win again. I'm on a mission. For Johnny's college fund."

"Oh…" There was no doubt that she was disappointed when he didn't mention the double-wide trailer. "That'll be nice for him, Cody."

He nodded. "I have to get ready to ride. You'd better go. Good to see you again."

"Don't treat me like a stranger, Cody."

"I don't know what you are to me anymore."

"I'd like to work through our problems."

"You have the problem. Remember? I can't do anything about my reputation rubbing off on you and Johnny. You have to deal with that.

So you decide what you're going to do. How you're going to handle it."

She touched his cheek lightly, and he felt as if his heart was going to jump out of his chest. "I'd better go."

"Good idea," he said quietly.

He waited until she was gone, took a breath and put his shirt back on.

He hadn't cut her any slack, but he didn't feel bad about that. She had some thinking to do. Either she was part of the crowd who was with him, or with those who booed him.

It was time to ride bulls and to try to push thoughts of Steven Lindy and Laura and Johnny out of his mind—for now.

Yeah, right.

Cody didn't know how he stayed on Maximilian, but he assumed that it was from pure anger that he'd kept tamped down for a long time.

It was a sweet victory because Max had never been ridden before in thirty times out of the chute.

Three-quarters of the crowd gave him a standing ovation; the other quarter booed him.

He chuckled. *Not bad. My approval rating is getting better.*

His mother and Cindy were screaming and blowing him kisses. Below them, in the Duke box, the reaction was controlled from all except Johnny. His son was waving his cowboy hat in the air. In that Maximilian was a Duke bull and he'd just spoiled its record, he was sure that J.W. was chewing his cigar butt until it was a wet mess.

He hadn't known that Max was a bounty bull, either, until the arena announcers told the crowd before his ride. He received a bonus of thirty thousand dollars for riding him.

Not bad for eight seconds of work.

* * *

Laura hated to hear the boos that erupted from some of the crowd. How narrow-minded could people be?

But they didn't know him as she did. Cody was a good guy, a sweet guy, an honorable guy.

Throughout grammar school and high school, he had always protected the underdog. Cody always confronted bullies, sometimes to his own detriment, but he didn't care.

It took a lot to get him riled. He always tried to reason with the attackers, but when that failed, he sprang into action.

And this time, it had resulted in broken ribs, stitches and bruises.

Laura's stomach roiled.

The announcers were making a big deal out of Cody's black eyes, broken ribs and stitches. They kept saying that they didn't know what happened—that it didn't happen from a bull—that Cody must have been hit by a freight train, or you should see the other guy, or a dozen other wisecracks.

Sheesh. Why couldn't they shut up?

With a couple exceptions, the other riders left Cody alone. He wasn't enjoying the easy camaraderie that the other cowboys were, and that bothered her, too.

"Cody Masters is cleaning up," J.W. said to Penny. "Who would have thought that? With all that bounty money and a ninety-two-point ride on Max, he's probably going to win today's round and the event. That'll be another thirty grand."

Laura smiled, thinking that Cody would have a sixty-thousand-dollar day. And he'd won twenty-one thousand yesterday. He could make a lot of improvements on the Double M with that kind of money.

Or Johnny could have it for college.

But she wanted that trailer with Cody. The man she'd loved all of her life.

Chapter Fourteen

"You won the whole thing, Mr. Masters. You have to be the bestest bull rider in the whole world," Johnny said, walking Pirate around the corral.

Cody laughed. "I just got lucky, son." He said the word without thinking.

"You probably won a zillion dollars."

Cody grinned. "Not quite." But he had won about one hundred thousand over the course of the three days. He cleaned up, which didn't endear him to the other riders.

Nothing could endear him to the other riders, anyway. They acted as if he carried some fatal disease.

By the time the gold buckles were awarded on Sunday, there were barely any people in the stands to watch.

It bothered him. He couldn't deny that, but the checks were already deposited in his account, which had had a sickly eighty-two bucks in it before.

"Go ahead and canter, Johnny. Remember what I told you."

He did a fabulous job, and Cody was so proud. Johnny was smart, kind to animals and a natural horseman.

In a half-hour, he was going to take Johnny on a little trail ride across the desert on an easy trail that Cody knew. The trail led to a dense mesquite-and-cactus forest and then to the highway, but they wouldn't be going that far.

Cody brought his own horse from the Double M, Midnight Blue, since he didn't want to be accused of using the Duke horses for pleasure.

He'd called Laura earlier and told her what he wanted to do and got it okayed by her. That was only after he promised that Johnny wouldn't be hurt.

Damn. Did she think he wouldn't take care of his son? He'd lay down his life for the boy.

He thought about inviting her to go along—Laura was an excellent rider—but he could tell he'd interrupted some kind of meeting.

So he rode Midnight Blue, and Johnny was at his side on Pirate. Cody opened the gate of the corral, and they were off walking.

Johnny couldn't wait to canter.

"Not yet. I'll tell you when," Cody said.

Johnny pointed out every bird, cactus, tree and wildflower that he encountered. He kept up a sweet chatter until Cody gave the word.

"You can canter now. Go ahead of me so I can watch your form."

The little boy's helmet bobbed up and down as he tried to concentrate on his riding.

Cody grinned. He loved watching him.

"Okay. Time to canter. Go for it."

"Yee-haw!" Johnny said. He liked this the best. So did Cody.

"Yee-haw!" Cody answered back.

When Cody saw the mesquite forest ahead, he yelled, "Okay, slow down and walk Pirate!"

Johnny did as he was told. He had perfect control over the reins and his feet.

"Excellent, Johnny. You're quite the cow-boy."

His face lit up. "Thanks!"

Cody wished that Laura could have seen him, could have been with them.

"You know, Johnny, we're going to have to get your mother and go on a trail ride and have a picnic so she can see you ride. You're doing an excellent job."

"Cool. Really cool," he said. "I'd like it if my mom could come."

"I'll make it happen," Cody said.

Four days later, Laura had paid particular attention to her appearance for her trail ride with Cody and Johnny. She wore her comfortable old Wranglers with just the correct amount of fading and wear, along with a long-sleeved blouse in a bright shade of peach that she tucked into her jeans and jazzed up with a silver concho belt. She had Arizona peridots dangling from her ears, new black and white snakeskin boots and a white cowboy hat.

She'd decided to pass on gloves, even though she'd just had a manicure.

She and Clarissa had made a picnic lunch complete with cold fried chicken, thermoses of lemonade and lots of cookies. Laura had packed everything into her saddlebags.

This was going to be fun. She hadn't been on a trail ride in years. Matter of fact, the last time was with Cody before he was arrested. Those were great days, a lot of fun. Somehow, they always ended up in the creek, laughing and making plans for their future together.

But they were only kidding themselves.

She sighed. She'd alienated Cody, made him feel even more like a pariah. But what could she do? She wasn't as strong as he was. She couldn't stand being gawked at, pointed at, and called names or publically shunned in some shape or form.

Even though others didn't, she still remembered that Cody had saved her life and the lives of three hundred others.

She wanted to talk to him about going to the Citizen of the Year ceremony. The award would go a long way in making people remember what he did, risking his own life in the process.

He needed to attend.

She smiled as she noticed how Johnny was concentrating on keeping his heels down.

She couldn't believe what progress Johnny had made under Cody's guidance.

"You're doing wonderful, Johnny. Nice riding!" she said.

"Mr. Masters said that I'm going to be a good cowboy. He's a good cowboy right now. I want him to teach me how to ride bulls."

Cody winked at Johnny. "You already are on your way. You start with sheep, and then work your way up. Got it? But we could do a little practice on your grandpa's sheep and travel to an event. That is, if it's okay with your mother."

Johnny's face was beaming. How could she say no to anything this little boy asked her for?

"Practice on the sheep with Mr. Masters, and we'll see."

"Okay, Momma! Cool!"

Maybe the boy would forget about riding bulls. She couldn't endure what she went through with Cody every time Johnny rode something.

"Mr. Masters is rich now 'cause he won the bull riding," Johnny blurted. "Are you as rich as my grandpa?"

Cody laughed. "No, son. I'm not."

Johnny said, "Uh…Mr. Masters, are you my daddy?"

Laura and Cody exchanged glances, and Laura tried to find her voice.

"Sweetie, what makes you ask that?"

"Sometimes, he calls me 'son.'"

"I see."

She met Cody's gaze, and judging by the expression on his face, he was hoping that she'd finally tell Johnny. She'd like to, but this wasn't a good time with all of them on horseback.

This topic needed further discussion when they all could sit and look at each other and talk.

The immediate problem was what she should tell Johnny.

By the time they reached the mesquite forest, he'd forgotten about his question. Deciding to have their picnic soon, Cody suggested they let their horses get water in a little stream that he knew about, which was located just inside the forest. The stream flowed from the hot spring down to the bigger creek that was their secret meeting place.

However, due to the severe rain that they'd had last night, the little stream was now a river. It was flowing gently right now, so Cody and Laura didn't worry much about it.

The horses enjoyed their water, and Cody had brought them carrots and apples as treats.

Then the three of them settled on a red blanket that Laura had brought.

Laura enjoyed Johnny's excited chatter about galloping and how he might be a jockey and "race in circles." Then he was going to be a bull rider, a firefighter and a police officer.

After lunch, Johnny laid down on the blanket, still talking a blue streak. Suddenly, he was quiet, and sleeping.

"Were you going to tell him about me, Laura?"

"Not today. I'm still waiting."

"For hell to freeze over?"

"For a good opportunity."

Cody took off his hat and raked his fingers through his jet-black hair. "Seems to me that it would have been a great opportunity to answer his question when he asked it just a little while ago."

"I think I want to tell my parents first."

"Name the time and place. I'll be there by your side."

"It won't be pretty," she said.

"That's an understatement." He put his hat back on and pushed it back with a thumb. "We keep having the same conversation over and over again. It doesn't seem to me that we are moving forward."

"I know. Just bear with me."

"You know I won a ton of money, Laura."

"I know. You ran away with the weekend."

"There's enough for a double-wide and the foundation to put it on, septic, wiring and the rest. I can even fix the barn roof. I even have a nice spot picked out at the Double M for us, if you can accept the consequences of being with me."

"Cody, I—um… I don't want to hurt you, but—"

"Say no more," he snapped. "I won't bug you about marrying me again. I, uh… When I've completed my parole, I think I'll be leaving here. Johnny won't need my money—not when J.W. is on the scene. I think I'll give it to my mother, and I'll head out. All I ask is that we arrange visitation somehow so I can see Johnny, and take him with me sometimes."

"Where will you go?"

"Someplace where they've never heard of Duke Springs and Cody Masters."

"Cody, just give me more time."

He didn't answer her. He got up and walked toward the river.

The trail ride lost all of its fun. As far as Cody was concerned, he was better off at the Arabian barns, training the horses there.

He could really get used to these well-heeled clients who didn't know a thing about horses but wanted an animal with good bloodlines and a hefty price tag just to show off.

He got along with them all and didn't mind if they watched him train their horses. From what he could tell, J.W.'s fancy cottages were always filled and the gourmet chef that worked in the "cookhouse" was always busy.

Laura was around all the time. She was courting a lot of them for the Duke Fund. She was perfect for that kind of thing—personable, beautiful, sincere, and she could easily part them from their money. He'd seen her in action many times.

The two of them acted like strangers. Conversations were strained, personal space was protected, and whenever he walked in her direction, one of them took a detour.

For two people who were in love, things certainly had changed.

Cody's heart was broken. It was his love for Laura that had kept him going for many years, through high school and prison.

He'd like to think it was the same for her. She'd had an overbearing father and mother. He'd had a beloved father who died way too early and a stepfather who was an abuser.

Life, huh? This couldn't be all there was.

But he did have Johnny.

While he was training another Arabian, J.W. came to watch. Cody was putting the horse through his paces, and J.W. liked to monitor the progress that the beautiful animals were making.

J.W. yelled to him to come to his office when he was finished.

Now what?

Dutifully, Cody walked to the B barn, knocked on J.W.'s office door and was told to come in. His parole officer was there, too.

"Hi, Officer Charles." Then it hit him. Because he'd been so damn busy, he hadn't reported to Officer Charles's office over in Phoenix.

"Uh-oh. I've been a little busy. I absolutely forgot to report. I've been working around the clock and—"

Officer Charles raised an eyebrow. "Riding bulls, going on trail rides, and you've been—"

"He's been saving lives." Laura walked in. "He saved my life and three hundred others. I'm sure you've heard about it."

"Actually, I have. And although you're supposed to report to me as part of your conditions of release, I've been keeping track of you through your mother and through Mr. Duke."

"I'm not a kid. You could have called me," Cody said.

"I could have, but they give me the collateral contacts I need to rack up to supervise you. State requirements, you know.

"But anyway, from now on, you must report every other week and tell me what you've been doing, unless I see you here. Then I'll excuse you."

"Yes, sir," Cody said.

"I can even forget about your failure to report on one condition."

"What's that?"

"That you go to that dinner and accept your Citizen of the Year award."

"Aw…hell."

Parole Officer Charles grinned. "The sheriff called me and they really want your butt there. It's the least you can do."

Laura stepped forward. "I'll accompany him and make sure he goes, Officer Charles."

"No way." J.W. shifted his cigar. "That's not necessary, Laura."

"Sure it is, Dad. It's the least I can do for the sheriff."

"There'll be a lot of important people there. You don't want to be seen with Cody." J.W. bit down on his unlit cigar so hard that he had to spit a chunk of it into a wastebasket.

"I certainly wouldn't mind being seen with a hero, Dad. And Cody's a real hero. Besides, I'm sure that Georgianna and Cindy will be there, too. We can all sit together."

"What? Sit with whom? Laura, what are you saying?"

"I'm saying that I'm friends with Georgianna and Cindy, and we'll all sit together." Laura stood straight and stared J.W. right in the eyes. *Now,* that *was his Laura!*

Cody felt as if he needed to sit. He was saved by Officer Charles, and Laura just announced that she wouldn't mind being seen with him and that she was friends with his mother and sister.

What a difference a day makes. Cody wondered what had suddenly gotten into Laura for her to defend him so staunchly.

Parole Officer Charles stood. "I'd better get going. I have other stops to make."

Cody held out his hand. "Thanks so much. And I won't forget to report from now on."

"Good. See that you don't. And by the way, I already told the sheriff that you'd be at the awards. Seven this Friday night, and you might want to wear a suit." On that note, he left the room.

"I'll get the suit cleaned that I wore to jail," Cody said, thinking out loud.

"You will not, Cody. We're going shopping," Laura stated.

"Laura!" J.W. yelled. "I won't allow it."

"Dad, I didn't ask your permission. And I really feel that it would be appropriate if you and Mom also attended the event. After all, Cody is your employee. You should support him."

On that note, they both left J.W. stammering and sputtering.

Laura felt as if she were flying. She'd stood up for Cody, and for herself, and it felt good. She didn't know where she had gotten the guts suddenly, but she was happy that she still had them. They'd been dormant for way too long.

When she attended the awards night with Cody, she was going to look fabulous. Red. She was going to wear a red gown shimmering with Swarovski crystal beads. She'd wear her hair up and Cody wouldn't know what hit him.

But, yes. He needed to get a new suit.

She checked her watch. In a couple of hours, she was going to meet Cody at their spot. Just she and Cody. She was going to put Johnny to bed early at her parents' house. He'd had a long day and was overtired and cranky.

"I don't wanna go to bed," he snipped.

"You need to go to bed. You're tired."

"I want to stay up and watch bull riding on TV. Grandpa's watching it. I want to have popcorn and watch it with him."

"Grandpa can record it and you can watch it in the morning. Now, let's go, Johnny."

"No!"

Laura took him by the hand and walked him to his room. "Put your pajamas on. You're a big boy and have been putting on your own pajamas for a long time now, so don't make me do it."

"I'll do it myself!"

Her normally sweet child had turned into a monster. "Then do it."

He went to a dresser drawer and put on one of his superhero pajamas. "Those are nice," she said, trying to lighten the mood.

"I don't like them. I want another superhero."

"Then find a pair, Johnny."

"They're in the laundry."

"Then wear the first pair for now! For heaven's sake, Johnny, you're being impossible!"

"Am not!"

She bit back an "Are, too!"

He was slower to get ready for bed than drying cement. All she could think of was that she was missing precious time with Cody. "Do you want me to help you?"

"No!"

"Then move it."

She sat down on his bed and tried not to overreact. That wouldn't do either of them much good.

"I want Cody to be my father," he said.

"Mr. Masters."

"I want Mr. Masters to be my father."

"Johnny, not now. Please. Get some sleep and we'll talk about lots of things in the morning. Okay?"

"No! I wanna talk now." He yawned, but he wouldn't give up and lie down.

"Get into bed, please."

"Don't wanna."

She took him by the hand, threw the covers back on his double bed and led him to the side of it. Finally, he climbed in.

She tucked him in and pushed the hair back from his face.

"Get some sleep, kiddo. You are totally over-tired."

He didn't answer her.

"Do you want to say some prayers together?" she asked.

He nodded. "You go first."

"God bless Grandma and Grandpa and Cindy and Georgianna."

"And Pirate," he added.

"Yes. Who else?"

"And Momma and Cody… I mean, Mr. Masters. And my turtle named Tommy."

"Yes, Tommy the Turtle. Bless him."

"And tell God that I really want Mr. Masters to be my father."

"Johnny…."

"Tell him."

"Dear God, Johnny really wants Cody Masters to be his father. Amen."

"Amen," Johnny said. "Can we ask Mr. Masters in the morning to be my father?"

Laura sighed. Her son had a one-track mind. "I don't think so. Now, go to sleep."

"No! I want to talk to Mr. Masters right now."

"Shush! Close your eyes and go to sleep." She put out the light and closed the door.

"No! I want a daddy. I want to talk to Mr. Masters right now." She could hear Johnny crying himself to sleep and her heart broke.

Chapter Fifteen

Cody was already at their secret spot, sitting on the big rock.

Laura raced into Cody's arms. "I'm so sorry for everything. For every asinine thing I said and did. I'm not embarrassed to be seen with you. I love you, Cody."

"I love you, too, but why the sudden change?"

"It finally hit me that Johnny needs a father. You should have heard him begging me to let you be his daddy."

"He did?"

"Yes. He did."

"And I didn't like how you were treated at the bull riding, and that I was treating you just like them—the only thing I wasn't doing was booing you. And then I was thinking about how you wanted to win money for our double-wide, and how you put your life on the line after being away from riding in such a long time. And how you are so good to Johnny, and you work so hard. Am I going to throw that all away for people like Cricket and mopes like the school board?"

"I'm glad you're now on my side, Laura. I really am."

"I've been such an idiot."

"Yeah, maybe…" He chuckled and held her tighter, running his fingers through her hair.

She clung to him—her Cody—like her future happiness depended on never letting this good man go.

"I want to make love with you, Cody," she whispered. "It's been so long."

He winked. "Just what I was thinking. Did you bring a blanket?"

"Sure did."

She went over to their usual spot and shook out the blanket, letting it drift to the ground. She held out her hand and he took it, lowering them both.

Pulling her onto him, he swept his hands over her back, then under her blouse. Soon he dispensed with the blouse and her bra altogether. His shirt joined hers on the corner of the blanket.

When she moved over him, he couldn't stop running his hands all over her body. Was this real? Or was this what he'd been dreaming about for such a long time?

He straddled her, unzipping her jeans, then his. Those came off along with underwear, and they were totally naked under the Arizona moon.

"You're beautiful, Laura. Just beautiful."

"So are you, Cody. You're leaner and more muscular." She looked down. "And bigger and thicker than I remember." She chuckled.

He laughed. "Flattery, huh?"

They kissed and played and laughed, and when they both couldn't wait any longer, he quickly rolled a condom down his length and entered her. She arched her back and squeezed him with her inner muscles, visibly enjoying every inch of him as he moved in and out of her.

He waited until she came, then released himself and held her in his arms, looking up at the moon, giving thanks for everything that he had.

The siren went off on the Duke Ranch. It was the signal for all hands and anyone who could hear it to head to the ranch as soon as possible.

Cody jumped to his feet, putting on his clothes and handing Laura hers.

"Something's wrong up at your ranch. Hurry."

"Oh, no! My father…he's been heading for a heart attack."

She buttoned her blouse on the run. Cody didn't care who saw them emerge together from the trail. The siren didn't go off for just anything, and some things were just more important than the two of them sneaking around.

Georgianna and Cindy came running, too.

"What is it? What's wrong?" Georgianna asked.

"Don't know yet," Cody said, running ahead of them to where J.W. stood on the porch.

J.W. looked like a train wreck, and Penny was crying.

"It's Johnny!" Laura said, reaching for Cody's hand. "Where's Johnny, Dad?"

"Johnny's missing," he said in a booming

voice to all those gathered around. "His…little footprints lead straight to the desert."

"Laura and I can find him," Cody said. "I took him on a trail ride through the desert. He might be on that trail."

She shook her head, tears trailing down her cheeks. "Go. I'd just hold you back."

"J.W., divide the volunteers up," Cody instructed. "Have some take the area by the Arabian barns going east. Some by the highway going north. Laura and I will be south." He turned to her. "I want you with me." Then he turned back to the volunteers who'd gathered. "We need to search by the Double M, too. Mom, you lead that crew. Penny, you take the area around the ranch house. Everyone, click the siren on if you find him. And J.W., get that helicopter over here that you used before and have the pilot search from the sky. I know that cell reception is pathetic around here, but keep your phones on anyway." Cody caught his breath, then added, "And don't forget flashlights, water and blankets. And go in threes. We don't want anyone else lost."

If J.W. was ticked that Cody was dishing out orders instead of him, he didn't show it. Instead, he nodded, taking Cody's instructions to heart.

Cody and Laura hurried off to find horses in J.W.'s remuda. Cody would rather have Midnight Blue, but it'd take too much time to run back to his ranch and saddle up.

He'd never saddled and bridled a horse so fast in his life. He took a gelding by the name of Hulk that he'd trained, and Laura saddled her horse, a pretty white quarter horse that she'd named Snow.

"Get supplies, Laura. I'll finish with Snow."

"Okay."

"Don't cry. Just hurry. It's going to be cold in the desert tonight."

"I know." She hurried back with a saddlebag and flung it over Snow's saddle.

"Let's go find our son, Laura." Cody took off at a trot out of the barn, then galloped. He knew this desert by heart, and he knew he could handle the terrain in the dark without jeopardizing Hulk.

Laura galloped behind him until the trail opened up, then she held her own next to him. He stole a look at her, and he could see that her cheeks were wet with tears.

"We'll find him, sweetheart. We'll find him."

Fifteen minutes later, Cody asked, "What's that?" He pointed to an object in the middle of the path. He dismounted to check it out.

"That's Johnny's stuffed bear Freddy!"

Relief lessened the tightness in his body. "Johnny can't be far from here. We're on the right track."

They could hear the chopper overhead. The

searchlight was aiming at the mesquite woods and then along the highway, but then it dipped and moved south.

"It looks like the chopper didn't see anything in the mesquite woods, but I'd bet a paycheck that he's in there—near where we had our picnic."

"Let's go, Cody."

Since the helicopter noise moved away, they'd be able to hear Johnny if he was near, so they shouted his name.

Then listened. Nothing.

"Johnny! Where are you?" Laura yelled.

"Johnny, answer us. Where are you?" Cody cried.

Cody got off his horse and handed the reins to Laura. "Stay here. Let me go on foot. This place is like a maze."

"No, wait! Let me go with you! I'm his mother."

"I'm his father, and I don't have time to argue

with you. Trust me. I need you to wait here. Okay?"

"Okay. Okay." She tossed him the saddlebag. "Be careful of snakes. And spiders. And other night animals. Bring Johnny out of there, Cody."

Laura turned her flashlight off to save the battery. As she sat on Snow in the dark, she thought she was going to have a meltdown.

The two people she loved most in this world were in the creepiest woods on the Duke property. Mesquite and cactus fought for the little sunlight that filtered through.

Cody was betting that Johnny was in there. So was she. If he was someplace else, they would have wasted a lot of time. Johnny would be cold and could be hurt, and she hoped that he'd put on some kind of shoes.

Come on, Cody. Hurry! Find our little boy!

"Johnny, where are you?" she yelled. "Johnny!"

Maybe if he was walking around, he would hear her.

She'd been a fool. She should have told Johnny that Cody was his father when Cody got out of jail. With a long explanation, if the other kids teased him, maybe Johnny wouldn't be ashamed.

She certainly could have told Johnny tonight after he kept begging her. That's why he was so restless and miserable. He'd wanted an answer.

Maybe even Johnny sensed the connection between Cody and himself.

She dismounted from Snow due to the coyotes she heard howling and held on to his and Hulk's reins. She didn't want the horses to take off.

"Cody! Cody, where are you?" she yelled.

"I'm still looking for Johnny."

Her heart sank. She'd hoped that Cody would answer that he'd found the boy.

The coyotes were getting closer, and she thought she saw a wolf. She wished she'd brought her gun. Instead, she shone her flashlight in a circle around her.

She burst into fresh tears. Johnny had to be scared out of his mind.

"Johnny! Cody! Answer me."

Why didn't Cody answer her?

"I have Johnny and we're coming out. Notify your father."

She pulled out her cell phone. No signal.

"Is Johnny okay?"

"He'll be fine."

Something was wrong with him, or else Cody wouldn't have said that. "What's wrong?" she yelled.

"All's fine."

Finally, they walked out of the forest. Dragging along the horses, she hurried to them, but she couldn't see them without shining the flashlight on them and into their eyes.

"Mommy," Johnny said weakly, holding out his arms for her to pick him up.

She gathered him up, and he clung to her. "Honey, are you okay?"

"My ankle hurts. I sat in the woods. And I was scared. And there was this big lizard thing, but I scared it off with a rock. And then the coyotes…"

"I know, honey. I know." She sniffed. "What were you thinking? You scared everyone."

"I—I wanted to run away."

"Why, Johnny?"

"Because I wanted to find Mr. Masters and ask him to be my father."

Laura handed Johnny back to Cody. "Johnny, Cody *is* your father. He's really your father, and he loves you. He really, really loves you."

She felt as if she'd lost twenty pounds of worry from her shoulders. There were still another twenty pounds left in the form of her parents. But Johnny seemed okay. That's all that mattered right now. "Are you really my dad?" Johnny asked, staring into Cody's eyes.

"I sure am," Cody said.

"Where've you been?" Johnny asked, holding his palms up and scrunching up his shoulders.

Cody chuckled. "It's a long story, and we'll tell you, but not right now. We have to tell everyone who's been searching for you that you're okay, so we'd better get going."

"Okay. Are Grandpa and Grandma mad at me?"

"No. They're worried," Laura said.

Cody mounted his horse and held out his hands. "How about riding with me, Johnny?"

"Okay...Dad."

Whoa! That little three-letter word packed a lot of punch.

Cody sat Johnny in front of him on the saddle. "Are you ready, Johnny?"

"Ready!"

"Are you ready, Laura?"

"Ready. Let's go!"

After a while, Cody asked, "Feel like galloping, Johnny?"

"Sure!"

"Tell me if it hurts your ankle, and we'll slow down. Okay?"

"Okay...Dad."

Cody hurried to the Dukes' ranch house. They didn't say anything else, due to the pounding of Hulk's hooves and the blowing of his breath.

He hugged his son close to him.

Laura trailed behind, trotting slower.

Cody slowed Hulk down and trotted right to the ranch house. His mother, Cindy, Penny and J.W. were standing there on the porch. Everyone looked distraught until they saw that he had Johnny.

J.W. punched the button of the siren, and then

hurried down the stairs. He held up his arms and took Johnny from him.

J.W. was about to cross-examine Johnny, but Cody shook his head no. Dismounting from Hulk, he walked toward J.W. and took Johnny back from him.

The man was about to say something, but Cody jumped right in.

"Uh… J.W., can you get that chopper back here? Johnny should be checked at the hospital. And make it fast. He might have a broken ankle, and there was talk about a big lizard."

"I shot a stone at it, and it went away, Grandpa. It didn't bite me," Johnny explained.

"Good. You're very brave, but it won't hurt to have you checked out," Cody said.

"I called the helicopter, Laura," J.W. said. "Told him to come back to the house and take Johnny to the hospital."

Georgianna and Penny had their arms

threaded around each other's waist. That was amazing. The two grandmothers.

Georgianna knew that Cody was Johnny's father, but he was pretty sure that Penny didn't have a clue.

The chopper landed on the Dukes' expansive lawn, and everyone ran to meet it.

"I can only take two, plus the little boy," said the pilot. "That's all."

"I'm Johnny's mother," Laura said.

Before she could say anything else, J.W. was ready to enter the chopper right behind her.

Laura turned to him. "Sorry, Dad, but Cody is Johnny's father. He gets to go."

"What did you say?"

"Cody Masters is Johnny's father. I'll talk to you later, but we have to go now. Let's go, Cody."

He'd never loved her more.

Cindy gave a squeal, or was that Penny?

"J.W., I'll give you all a call after Johnny is checked out," Cody said, closing the door.

"Let's go," he said to the pilot, feeling that they should rush to the hospital, but on the other hand, he was pretty sure that Johnny wasn't bitten. He'd be showing signs of distress by now, but he did want to have his son's ankle checked out.

Johnny sat in between Laura and Cody on the backseat of the chopper. He shared Laura's seat belt. Cody held his hand, but he could tell that Johnny was excited to go on this little adventure.

It took less than a half hour to get to the hospital. Nurses and other medical personnel were waiting on the helicopter pad. They had a wheelchair for Johnny.

"It's his ankle," Laura said, "But he was lost in the desert. We'd like him checked out head to toe, please."

"Got it," said one of the nurses. "We'll take him to X-ray and check him out there."

"Thanks," Laura said.

"Follow us."

They took the elevator down to the emergency room at the Duke Springs Hospital. Then they wheeled Johnny through a set of double doors.

"Have a seat in the waiting room. We'll call you when Johnny's ready," the nurse said.

"Will do," said Cody.

They sat in the waiting room and held hands.

"Don't worry, honey," Cody said. "He'll be fine. If he was bitten by anything, he'd show symptoms, and I would have taken care of it. Besides, he said he threw a rock at the lizard." He chuckled. "That's my boy!"

Laura squeezed his hand. "I'm glad you're with me, Cody."

"I'm glad, too." He kissed the palm of her

hand. "And I'm glad you told J.W. that I'm Johnny's father."

"I should have done it a long time ago, but I needed you with me. It was only right. I'm ready for us to be a family. You have money now, and I can match it from my savings, so we'll have a nice nest egg to start out in that double-wide."

"Are we still putting our home on the Double M?" Cody asked.

"I think we should get our own land, something that's really ours, but I don't want it too far away. Johnny needs family around him, and he'll have it—two grandmothers, a grandfather and Aunt Cindy, a mom and a dad and Clarissa. He'll miss Clarissa if we go too far away."

"Sounds like a plan," Cody said.

"Finally, we are going to be a family." Laura rubbed her thumb on the back of Cody's hand.

A man in scrubs came into the waiting room. "My name's Rodney McGlaskin, but call me

Rod. I'm an X-ray tech. I just want to tell you that Johnny is okay. No bites or anything, some scratches, but he was loaded with tiny cactus needles, like from a prickly pear. We took care of them and doused him with antiseptic. The good news is that the X-ray doesn't show any trauma to the ankle. He might have twisted it a bit, so he should probably go easy on it for a while. You know, he's a cute kid."

"Yes, he is," Cody said.

"So, he's all set. But you need to go to the first floor and give them some information. Then feel free to leave."

He paused as Johnny was brought out in a wheelchair. Laura went over and hugged him. Cody followed suit.

"How are you all going to get home?" Rod asked. "Taxis aren't running this time of night, and if they were, they wouldn't go way out to the Duke Ranch."

"If I know my father and mother, they'll be downstairs waiting for us," Laura said.

Cody grinned. "And I'll bet that my mother and Cindy are with them."

"I hope they have a van," the man said.

"They do," Laura said.

Cody pushed Johnny's wheelchair to the elevator and saw all the pictures of the Duke family forefathers on the wall, all the way back to a tintype of Elijah Duke in 1834 with his wife, Laura.

"Were you named after her?"

"Yes. So I hear, but there were a couple of Lauras on my mother's side, too."

"The Masters only settled here in 1867, a bit after the Civil War ended."

"We were all pioneers here."

Cody snapped his fingers. "I know exactly where my ancestors first settled. The original homestead stood right where my mother's house is now. That's why my father was so thrilled to get the land back from J.W. He said that he never should have sold it in the first place."

"When we get married, I think we should live exactly in the middle of both places!"

Cody's eyes twinkled. "Why, Laura Elaine Diane Duke, are you asking me to marry you?"

"I sure am."

"Yee-haw!" said Johnny.

Chapter Sixteen

Five months later, everyone was sitting around the Dukes' patio table discussing the wedding, when J.W. pushed a stack of papers into the middle of the table.

J.W. grinned. "Laura and Cody, here's our wedding present to you. It's from Georgianna and Penny and me with our love."

J.W. pushed the thick document toward them. Laura picked it up. "What is it, Dad? It'll take us forever to read."

"She's right, J.W. Allow me to explain,"

Georgianna said, taking a deep breath. "It's the deed to a parcel of land that straddles both the Duke Ranch and the Double M. We had everything resurveyed, and this is yours, if you'd like it, that is."

"What about the fence?" Cody said.

"The fence is coming down," Penny replied, putting her hand over Cody's. "In more ways than one."

"Thank you, J.W., Penny, Mom. We gratefully accept." Cody held out his hand to shake J.W.'s, and J.W. hesitated just a split second, then he grabbed Cody's hand and shook it.

So okay, he was still absorbing the whole thing. He'd get used to having him as a son-in-law eventually, but J.W. had come a long way since Cody was first released from prison.

Georgianna and Penny had buried the hatchet since the night of Johnny's disappearance. Suddenly, they were the best of pals and lived to shop and buy things for their grandson and plan the wedding.

The wedding reception was to be held at the Duke Springs Country Club. Cody protested about the huge crowd, but Laura and the Dukes felt that it'd be a good opportunity for everyone to see how happy they both were.

Cody had made good on his promise to go to the awards night for citizen of the year. Almost every attendee congratulated him, and maybe he'd made some headway into being accepted again by the whole town.

Maybe the word got out that if J.W. and Penny Duke accepted him, then they should, too.

Cody guessed that it was one benefit about his fragile relationship with J.W. Laura was certainly more relaxed with her parents as time went by. Johnny just wanted everyone around him all the time, especially "Grandma Georgianna" and "Aunt Cindy Lou Who."

* * *

Four months later, the small wedding party posed for pictures on the patio of the Duke Ranch.

Cindy was beautiful as the maid of honor, and Slim Gonzalez was the best man, but Johnny stole the show as a very serious ring bearer with a totally important job.

After the photographer was done, Georgianna raised her hand to get everyone's attention.

"Before the ceremony starts, I'd like to invite you all to my home for refreshments." She made eye contact with J.W. and Penny. "I have another gift for Cody and Laura that I'd like you all to participate in."

Georgianna hugged Johnny. "Johnny, Clarissa will watch you for a while, then you can join us. She can show you the new kittens in my barn. Okay, sweetie?"

"Okay, Grandma," he said.

"Penny, J.W., I'd like to make sure you will come."

Penny nodded. "We'll be there."

J.W. made a grumbling noise, and Penny turned to him. "John Wayne Duke, get in that Cadillac and point it at the Double M."

"Yes, Penny."

Later, at the Double M, Cody noticed a couple of cars that he didn't recognize.

When they walked into the house, Cody saw that the other guests that Georgianna invited were the district attorney, the sheriff, his parole officer and Judge Carlton, who had sentenced him.

Oh, no. Not on his wedding day!

What was this about?

Soon, Georgianna formally introduced everyone.

J.W., Georgianna and Penny had all gone to school with them, with the exception of Cody's parole officer, and were reminiscing about old times in high school.

"What's going on, Mom?" Cody asked.

"Everyone, please get some refreshments first," she said. "Then take a seat at the table. I have something to say."

Georgianna passed around the coffeepot. Before them was a virtual buffet of danishes, donuts, cookies and fruit.

When everyone was seated and eating, she handed Laura and Cody a stack of legal-size paper.

But when Cody looked at the title on top—*Affidavit*—he stood. "Mom, no!" His face drained of color. "Don't you dare do this."

"It's time," she said. "It's my gift to you and Laura. It was a mistake from the beginning. The biggest mistake I ever made."

Georgianna turned to those sitting around the table. "You see, I let my son take the blame for a crime that I committed. I was the one who shot Hank Lindy. After he was done beating on me, he turned his attention to Cindy. Little ten-year-old Cindy. He was slapping her face and holding her down on the couch. She was struggling to get away and crying." Georgianna closed her eyes, then continued. "I got Mike's old rifle and shot him before he hurt her even more."

Georgianna wiped at her eyes. "Cody came into the room after the fact and guessed correctly what had happened. He said that Cindy would need me and that I just couldn't go to prison. He said that he'd take the blame. At the time, I thought he was right, but I've regretted that decision every second of every day, especially when I see how he's been treated by everyone in this town—like manure on their boots."

"That's enough, Mom," Cody said. "It was the only way out. Cindy did need you. She needed her mother."

Georgianna sighed. "Let me finish, Cody. So, last week, I met with these gentlemen and confessed. My confession is on those papers before you. Cody and Laura, this is my wedding gift to you. It'll be in the paper tomorrow, and I'll be arrested for falsely reporting an incident and manslaughter."

"The hell you will," Cody said.

There was silence throughout the room. No one moved.

Laura lifted her coffee for a sip, then put it down instead of drinking it. "Georgianna… um… Mom, Cody told me he was innocent, and I believed him. But then after I saw how people treated him, and it made me crazy. I didn't want that stigma and I didn't want it for Johnny. Then, as time went on and we got reacquainted, I realized that Cody was the same man that I always loved, and I didn't care what people thought." She looked at her parents.

"And I was tired of sneaking around. Cody—and Johnny—deserved better from me."

"Laura." Georgianna tapped her finger on the papers. "My affidavit will erase any stigma from Cody and you and Johnny. He'll have a clean slate."

"Mom, for heaven's sake, why didn't you talk to me first?" Cody asked.

"Because I knew what you would have said."

"I would have told you no!"

"Too late now. It's already done," Georgianna said. "Isn't it, Jeff?"

The district attorney nodded. "Yes. Your mother confessed to the murder of Hank Lindy and the whole cover-up. Actually, Georgie, I couldn't believe that you married him in the first place."

"I thought he was a nice guy," Georgianna said. "We had fun and a lot of laughs. I never, ever thought...that he'd beat us."

Judge Carlton cleared his throat. "And here's

our wedding gift to you, Cody and Laura… and you, Georgianna." He took a deep breath. "We have all discussed the matter and have decided that due to the extenuating circumstances…um…uh… Well, here's basically the story that's going into the newspaper."

Judge Carlton raised his index finger. "The real perpetrator who entered Georgianna's home came forward and confessed that he tried to rob her and Hank Lindy at gunpoint. The robbery was foiled by Cody Masters. When a fight over the gun ensued, Hank Lindy was accidentally shot by the robber, who escaped, and there's a warrant out for his arrest." He reached down and helped himself to a cheese danish. "It'll be tidied up, but that's the gist of it."

"Why are you doing this?" Cody asked.

"Because this was the most unselfish act we've ever experienced. And because we think that your mother had cause to stop Lindy in the course of a crime against herself and a minor child," said Sheriff Butler. "Georgie, if you'd told us the truth in the beginning, Cody would never have gone to jail. Neither would you."

"Cody, I'm so, so sorry," she said. "I just can't apologize enough to you."

"It's done, Mom. Stop. I lived through it," Cody said. He turned to the judge, the DA and the sheriff. "This is a wonderful wedding present. Thank you, all of you."

"The good news keeps coming, Cody," Penny said. "The headline of your wedding announcement in the morning paper will be Cody Masters, Hero, Marries Laura Duke."

"What? I get second billing?" Laura feigned that she was mad.

Penny laughed. "You're right, darling. I can flip it around."

"And the story about the intruder will be on the first page," said the sheriff.

"And when I get back to the office, I'll file for a discharge from parole for you, Cody." Parole

Officer Charles shook his hand. "It was nice to meet you. You're a good man."

They stood to go, but Cody wouldn't have it until he'd shaken everyone's hands and thanked them profusely.

Laura shook their hands after Cody and added heartfelt hugs. "I'd like to invite you all to celebrate with us, and we are really going to have fun! Please come to our reception at the country club," Laura said. "Please. And bring a guest. We'll have more than enough food."

With joyful tears, Georgianna hugged the three men, too. "I was all set to go to jail after the reception. Now everything is so…perfect!"

"I feel like an old fool. Can you two ever forgive me?" J.W. asked. "I wanted to make sure that Laura had a man who could support her in the style that I wanted for her, and that wasn't you, Cody. But Laura loves you. She's always loved you, in spite of my selfish attempts to keep you apart. All that time wasted…"

Cody shook his head. "It took Johnny's running away to finally wake up everyone. Just remember, J.W., I'm never going to be as rich as you, but I will love Laura and Johnny until the day I die."

"Oh, you'll be as rich as me, all right. I'm turning over the Arabian division to you two. Laura, I did wrong by never teaching you the family business. Now I'm going to rectify that."

"I still have things to do at the Double M," Cody said.

Georgianna shook her head. "You won't have much to do anymore. Now that I'm not going to jail, I'm going to give all my livestock to you two and finally retire from ranching. I'm going to try my hand at running a gift shop in town next to Penny's dress shop. Cindy is going to work there, too, after school. We'll feature our prickly pear jelly."

"What a day this has been already," Penny

said. "And we still have a wedding and a reception to attend!"

"Oh, it's only just begun." Laura grinned, taking Cody's hand. "Cody and I have a present for you all, too."

"What's that?" J.W. asked.

"You are all going to be grandparents again!" Laura said.

Cody laughed, just thinking about how he'd made love to Laura twice, and twice she'd gotten pregnant. He'd better build a really big house!

After the commotion and congratulations died down, Laura raised her and Cody's hands to the sky.

"Now, get me and my cowboy and our son to the church on time. We're finally getting married!"

* * * * *

MILLS & BOON®

Why shop at millsandboon.co.uk?

Each year, thousands of romance readers find their perfect read at millsandboon.co.uk. That's because we're passionate about bringing you the very best romantic fiction. Here are some of the advantages of shopping at www.millsandboon.co.uk:

* **Get new books first**—you'll be able to buy your favourite books one month before they hit the shops

* **Get exclusive discounts**—you'll also be able to buy our specially created monthly collections, with up to 50% off the RRP

* **Find your favourite authors**—latest news, interviews and new releases for all your favourite authors and series on our website, plus ideas for what to try next

* **Join in**—once you've bought your favourite books, don't forget to register with us to rate, review and join in the discussions

Visit **www.millsandboon.co.uk**
for all this and more today!